Chapter One

PARIS. DECEMBER 1947.

They say impoverished Italian Counts marry money; the heiress, on the other hand, marries for the title. There is never any question of undying love in the equation.

However, Rachel observed that this did not seem to be the case with Count Tristan Santinelli. He was plainly grieving over the loss of his beautiful bride – Countess Santinelli who had been found brutally murdered, two weeks ago, in an artist's studio in Montmartre. The papers had carried nothing but sensational news features related to the case ever since. There had been articles and editorials about the deplorable state of law and order in the city, features about a sudden increase in Parisian crime rate and interviews with her friends - high society ladies, who were feeling vulnerable and unsafe. So much so that the queen of Parisian nightlife, Madame Chartreuse gave the press a statement that she wouldn't be surprised, if she was found murdered in her bed one of these days. For a week and a half it seemed that the murderer, perhaps a mad man, was still running loose. Despite multiple arrests, the police were still clueless as to who had committed the ghastly act. Then they made a surprising arrest – they shackled the artist, Alexandre Dubois, in whose studio the crime was committed. The non-stop coverage in newspapers was only to be expected. After all, the victim had been an extraordinary woman - a charismatic, young and beautiful social celebrity.

Rachel had found her life's story fascinating. Countess Santinelli, erstwhile known as Sarah Hickson, had been the sole heiress to her millionaire father's flourishing Business Empire, which had started humbly with the manufacturing of Hickson's cough drops in England. In the past thirty years it had grown exponentially to encompass hundreds of manufacturing units across Allied Europe, including iron and steel, arms and ammunitions. Where Miss Hickson had lacked in aristocratic lineage, she had more than made up in looks. Apart from her well endowed bank balance, she had been widely acclaimed as a beauty of the first water.

Beauty is a strange thing and even the most highly acclaimed society beauties cannot hold a candle to the front-line dancers at the Moulin Rouge and in all probability would never make the cut, even if a twist of fate took them there. But then as in all professions, one must give the amateur a little more leeway. And in this cut-throat arena, society beauties by default need be classified under the amateur category. Sarah Hickson, on the other hand could have taken up the job at the Moulin Rouge anytime she set her mind to. The management would have rolled out the red carpet for her perfect hourglass figure, enhanced by the siren like beauty of her visage.

Painters tried to capture the masses of long devilish red curls that framed her Magdalene face and set off her startling emerald eyes. Composers wrote songs about her and even one of the most acclaimed writers of the time, despite his geriatric status, dedicated his romantic anthologies to her. Hers was not a timid or demure beauty, like that of a Madonna or Mona Lisa or the ephemeral women that Titian or Rubens painted. Her beauty was vibrant and alive, akin to the full-blooded beauties depicted in Rossetti's Proserpine and Monna Vanna, rumoured to have been inspired by Dante's poetry.

She had a flair for the dramatic and a joie de vivre that shone through the grainy black and white newspaper images and fired the imagination of the girl-on-the-street and the society hostess alike, and that made her unique.

Two years ago, just as the war in Europe had finally come to its weary end, Miss Hickson's father had passed away leaving the twenty-two year old Sarah, with a vast fortune and the dubious reputation of being one of the richest single women in the world. Instead of making a suitable match and settling down immediately, as her numerous stodgy yet well meaning English guardians and legal advisors expected of her, she surprised everyone by moving to Paris - the city she loved most and made a luxurious suite of rooms at The Ritz, her home. Moreover, much to the consternation of their conservative mindsets, she chose to live there in a state of un-chaperoned luxury.

Rachel had loved the idea of Sarah Hickson's independence and smiled to herself at the horror and grief she would have caused her mother, had she lived the same way. But then, she knew that vast wealth had that penultimate power to bestow freedom and independence, which transcended genders and the rigid morality of social conventions. It had been widely known that Miss Hickson had been one of the most sought after heiresses in Europe. After all, as Jeremy had pointed out to her, with some amusement that finding an heiress who didn't look like the back end of a motor bus, was akin to finding a four leafed clover in post-war Europe.

There was even some talk about her receiving a marriage proposal from a well known European Head-of-State. Through the war years, when she had lived in England, she had been a darling of the war time press. When she did a charity drive in London, the streets would be paved by admirers of both sexes. Rachel had never met her but like the rest of Europe, she knew that Sarah Hickson could have married just about anyone, up until she made the surprising match in Paris with the relatively unknown Italian Count.

The wedding had taken place a year ago. A lot of water had flown under the bridge since. Rumours about the marriage going south had started within six months of the low key wedding in France. In the past year, Rachel along with Jeremy had not kept track of the gossip columns as their time had been otherwise occupied in solving cases that seemed to fall pat in their laps. They had just wrapped up their third case. The investigation in the Riverton murder case had taken them all the way to India and on the way back they had gotten off the boat at Marseilles for a well deserved holiday at Paris. The plan was to spend two weeks in Paris and then head home to Rutherford Hall for a family Christmas.

But their stint at Paris was not what Rachel had hoped for. It rained constantly and the gloom in the sky seemed to reflect on the entire city. In addition, the fact that the newspapers carried nothing but articles on the murder, crime in general and the gloom and doom of the dissipated law and order situation in Paris, only added to the dismal atmosphere. Countess Santinelli's many friends and acquaintances were in mourning and the Parisian weather seemed to have followed suit. The past few days had seen steady sleet that lent a chill melancholy to the otherwise gay atmosphere of Parisian street life.

On this grey, wintry morning, Count Santinelli had braved the dismal weather to meet Rachel and Jeremy at 'Le Montebello' – a cafe with a view of Notre Dame and was currently seated across them, at a table inside that faced the plate glass windows. The interior was gloomy despite all the lamps being lit.

The Count – a tall, well built, young man in his late twenties had an angelic face, an aquiline nose, hazel brown eyes and brown ringlet curls that came down to the nape of his neck. He had walked into the cafe wearing a brooding look and a large black cloak, the latter of which he removed to reveal a beautifully tailored charcoal grey suit set off with a flamboyant paisley tie. Despite his apparent debonair charm, he had a certain swagger that belied the grace and fluidity of his movements and yet, strangely enhanced them. Rachel found him very good looking in a sophisticated yet rugged way.

The Count did not have any trouble in finding them. The cafe was not crowded and theirs' was one of the few occupied tables inside. The other one had a group of four boisterous American tourists.

The Count didn't waste any time. Once the perfunctory greetings were over, he came straight to the point and in his thick Italian accent said, 'I want you to find out who killed my wife.'

Jeremy nodded with a faint smile, 'Yes, we gathered as much over the telephone, but before we discuss that would you care for some coffee first?'

'No. No. First I want you to agree that you will take on my wife's case. I assure you, money is no object.'

'I'm sure it isn't but I'll be honest with you. Money has never been our motivation in solving cases. At the risk of sounding like a pompous old windbag, I'd say our primary motivation in our past three cases has been the quest for justice. On two occasions, if it wasn't for our intervention the wrong person would have been swinging at the gallows, on circumstantial evidence.'

Rachel interjected, 'It is true, Count Santinelli. We both strongly believe in the sanctity of life and abhor injustice. We don't take up cases unless there is some indication, a sign that our intervention is required. Besides, I'm sure that Jeremy already informed you over the telephone that we are here in Paris merely on a short holiday.'

The Count spoke with barely disguised impatience. 'Look, you have to help me. I have heard of you both from my friend, The Maharajah of Dharanpore.'

'Ah, that would be Prince Dickie. It is a small world indeed! We just got off the boat from India last week, at Marseilles.'

'I know. That is how I know you are in Paris. The Prince wired to tell me that I ought to ask for your help in this messy affair. He said that you both were my best hope under the circumstances. He told me what you had done for him in India and how Madame and you had solved the case, which no one else could in the past two years.'

Jeremy said with a smile, 'More Madame than me, really. I was just the bystander egging her on with moral support.'

'Jeremy, you know that isn't entirely true,' Rachel interjected with a grin.

'Darling, we both know it is, but that is neither here nor there.' Turning to the Count, he continued, 'Your wife's murder is a very high profile case. From all accounts, it seems to be an open and shut case. Even if it isn't, I am sure there are enough people investigating it already. Where do we come in?'

'Look, it may be so but they are investigating, how you say, in English – up the wrong tree! I need someone to conduct an enquiry on my behalf. You see, I had confided to Prince Dickie about my predicament just before he set sail for India. In his wire, he mentioned how you both can be relied upon to be discreet. It is my primary requirement, in this case.'

Rachel asked, 'Really, why?'

'Because I know who killed her!'

'Then why don't you go to the Préfecture de Police with your allegations?' Jeremy asked in an even tone.

'They would only laugh at me. It should be evident to you by now that I have no proof to support my belief.'

'And what is it you want us to do exactly?' Rachel asked.

'I want you to prove that my brother, Pietro, killed my wife!'

Chapter Two

'So what do you think, darling?' Rachel asked, putting her arm through Jeremy's, as they trudged along the cobblestoned streets. Their meeting with the Count over, they were making their way back to their charming little hotel overlooking the Seine. Walking towards Quai d'Anjou in Ile Saint Louis, Rachel realised that although the rain had stopped, it was still bitterly cold. The wind had picked up and it felt as though it was coming directly from the North Pole. Her teeth were chattering.

'It's not exactly an invitation to the royal ball, my dear. We need to take our time, you know. Find out more about this case. Weigh the pros and cons so to speak,' Jeremy said with a smile as he stopped walking, took his muffler off and wrapped it around her neck.

'Oh, thank you, darling. God! It's freezing. I should have listened to you and worn my thick ugly coat instead of this excuse for warmth that I have on,' she said grimacing, looking down at her smart Camel button down wrap. She had been carried away at the couturiers and spent a fortune on a new wardrobe. The smooth sales lady had exclaimed with delight at how Madame had effortlessly imbibed 'Parisienne chic.' That elusive *je ne sais quoi*. But Parisienne chic wasn't doing her much good at the moment.

Jeremy who had been married eight months by now - long enough to know the inevitable repercussions of 'I told you so', merely smiled beatifically as Rachel narrowed her eyes suspiciously at his new found reticence.

As they renewed their walk, Rachel continued, 'But Jeremy, we promised the Count we'd give him an answer by tomorrow evening.'

'Yes darling, but before we can do that, I think we ought to find out a little more about this case. I'll make a few calls. Luckily, over the years, I've worked with some very nice people up at La Sûreté Nationale and I still know a few investigating officers.'

'I keep forgetting what a resourceful man I married. But I never knew that the Scotland Yard and the Sûreté worked hand-in-glove. I thought we were always at loggerheads with the French – we won't learn their language and they refuse to learn ours, well, along with all the other fuss over decisions taken during the war.'

'Well, darling, the thing is when criminals from our end of the Channel make a dash for it, the Dover – Calais route is usually the first thing they seem to opt for.'

'Tsk, tsk. No sense of imagination.'

'None whatsoever. It's appalling. And it seems to work both ways, for some reason. So you see, we do have a sort of a necessary partnership with our brethren at La Sûreté. Besides, to be fair, the Sûreté is considered as 'La Mère' - the idea of Scotland Yard sprang from her in the first place.'

'Now you're having me on.'

'It is a recorded historical fact, my dear.'

'Care to enlighten me, Professor?' Rachel asked tongue-in-cheek.

Jeremy responded without missing a beat. 'Certainly. The Sûreté was founded over a hundred years ago, in 1812 to be precise, by a chap called Eugène François Vidocq. He was convinced that crime could not be controlled by the prevailing police methods at the time, so he organized a special branch of the criminal division modelled on Napoleon's political police.'

'Secret police, you mean. Like the modern day Gestapo?'

'I don't think they'd be very pleased with that comparison but in a way, I daresay you could be right because within eight years, by 1820, the astonishing thing was that although it was just a thirty man crime fighting unit, mostly working undercover, they managed to reduce the crime rate in Paris by a massive forty percent! Once that became widely known, other countries including ours followed suit. The Sûreté became the inspiration for crime fighting organisations the world over – Scotland Yard, Sûreté du Québec, the FBI, and so on.'

'That is very interesting.'

'What is even more interesting is that its early members consisted largely of reformed criminals.'

'Set a thief to catch a thief?' Rachel asked with a raised eyebrow.

'Précisément! Once we get back to the hotel, I think I ought to make a few calls and see if I can catch up with an old hand at the Sûreté - Henri Beauchamp. He's probably gone up the ranks since we last met. And while I do that, you could sit in front of the roaring fire they always seem to have going in the sitting room and thaw out a bit.'

'Sounds like an excellent plan, darling. Just what the doctor ordered. I just hope I'm not coming down with the wretched flu,' Rachel said miserably. Seconds later she sneezed into his muffler.

II

An hour later, Rachel was comfortably curled up on the chaise lounge in the sitting room, in front of a crackling log fire. She had a hot water bottle and a penny dreadful for company while Jeremy was at the historic 36, quai des Orfèvres or simply the 36, as locals called it. It was home to the headquarters of the Brigade Criminelle, or 'La Crim' - the oldest and perhaps most famous division of the Sûreté, in charge of homicide cases among other serious crimes.

After a long walk through several passages and ornate stairways, accompanied by a gendarme, he was shown into a room with high ceilings and ornate mouldings.

'Bonjour, Inspector Beauchamp, so good to see you again!' Jeremy said, as he walked towards the desk at the far corner of the room.

The man sitting at the desk rose. He was a tall, lanky man with floppy dark hair, brooding eyes and a characteristic stoop. But now his face was lit up with a genuine smile. 'Mon ami, Jeremy! Please, we still call each other with the first names, non?'

'Of course, Henri. You look just the same, old chap.'

'So do you. What brings you to Paris? I hear in the ivy that you left the Yard.'

'Ah yes, that must have been the grapevine then,' Jeremy responded with an understanding smile.

'Ah, yes. The grapevine, the ivy, they all climb eh?' He said laughingly.

'They certainly do, my friend,' Jeremy said, as the two men shook hands.

'My English, it improves daily,' Henri said with a dramatic hand gesture.

'I envy you mon ami, if only I could claim the same thing about my French!'

'Ah, je sais que tu parles francais assez bien!' Henri said, wagging a finger at Jeremy.

'Hardly! C'est très gentil à vous! Very kind, indeed. Personally I think my French is just about passable.'

'But you are not here to take French lessons, mon ami. Please to sit,' Henri said, offering a chair.

'Thank you, Henri. You are right about that,' Jeremy said as he sat in the visitor's chair across the desk. 'I came here to meet you and ask you if you'll help me make a decision. You see, I've been offered a private commission to investigate a case here in Paris.'

'Qu'est-ce que c'est? A criminal case?'

'Oui. You would probably know all about it even if you aren't personally investigating it. The Santinelli case?'

'Comment?' Henri shot back.

'I had better explain. We, that is, my wife and I got involuntarily involved in solving murder cases, not in a professional capacity you understand, but simply because we happened to be there when the crimes were committed and a natural curiosity got the better of us. The first was her maternal Uncle's murder – you may have heard of it.

The case did make waves last year – the Rutherford Hall murder?

'Oui! The lady, Mademoiselle Rachel, I think, she is your wife? That I did not know. But Monsieur, she is famous!'

'Well she was neither famous nor my wife at the time, but we did get married shortly after that.'

'La femme formidable!'

'She certainly is, Henri. I'd like you to meet her. I am sure you two would get along famously.'

'Oui. Certainement, it would be a great plaisir to meet Madame Richards!'

'Oh, she's not Madame Richards. She has progressive ideas, you see, like many modern young girls these days. And she has kept on her maiden name after marriage - Markham.'

'And you are fine with that, mon ami?'

'Well, I haven't much choice in the matter, Henri, but if I did I'd have personally encouraged her to take whichever name she wanted to, as long as she was comfortable with it.'

'You are a strange man, Jeremy.'

'No, not really. But our marriage is. You see when we took our wedding vows we promised each other that our marriage would be one of equal partnership and I agreed with her that if I didn't have to take on her last name, there was no good reason for her to take on mine simply because we decided to live as man and wife.'

'Ah, well, these times, they change us eh? The war has changed our cities, why not the people, the way we think, eh?'

'Quite!'

'And you were saying, Madame and you got involved in that murder case in a, how you say, non professional capacity?'

'Yes but there's more. That was just the first. The second one was the Ravenrock case six months ago at Dartmouth in Devon. I don't suppose you would have heard about that all the way here in Paris but it made quite a splash in our dailies, on the other end of the Channel, I can tell you that. We caught a serial killer and in the process Rachel nearly got killed herself.'

'Non!'

'Yes! And I thought as any normal person would that after yet another near death experience like that she wouldn't be in a hurry to experience a brush with the pearly gates just yet but I was wrong. What can I say? She seems to have a woman's knack for getting into trouble. And if that wasn't enough, my erstwhile boss, Chief Inspector Harrow at Scotland Yard took a shine to her and involved both of us in a third case! That too, in a Maharajah's palace in India. We just got back from there.'

'You solved that as well?'

'I had very little to do with it. The credit goes to her entirely for cracking that one. Like I said, she seems to have an uncanny knack for this sort of thing and she's remarkably good at getting the truth out of people. I must admit that she solved the third one with very little help from me.'

'And now she wishes to solve the Santinelli case? But I think she will be disappointed, non? We already solved it.'

'Really? If you ask me, I think that's a bit of luck for us. As long as you can keep Count Santinelli off our backs.'

'How is it that you know the Count?'

'We don't. You see, we met him for the first time this morning. It seems the Indian Maharajah – Prince Dickie – the one we solved the last case for, is an old friend of the Count's. To cut a long story short, the prince wired and informed him that we were in Paris. Hence the meeting. And at this meeting, the Count absolutely insisted that we poke about. Apparently he is convinced that you haven't got the right man.'

'Non. We have not got a man at all,' Henri said with a shake of his head.

'But the papers say that the artist Alexandre Dubois was arrested the day before.'

'We now know that it is not the artist Dubois but his mistress Suzette who killed the Countess. Inspector Didier Lachaille – you remember him? He is in charge now.'

'Vaguely. I don't think we ever worked together. And Inspector Lachaille is certain that Dubois' mistress is responsible?'

He shrugged. 'She has the motive and no alibi and she does not deny it.'

'Hmm. But correct me if I'm wrong. The Countess was found with her throat slit.'

'Oui. Ear to ear. Horrible,' Henri said, making a motion across his throat. 'I saw the body when it was brought in.'

'Hard to believe a woman could have done it. Stabbing is more in a woman's line, don't you think.'

'Ah, yes but with le crime passionelle, one can never say,' Henri said making a theatrical gesture.

'I say, Henri, would you mind terribly putting in a good word for me with Inspector Lachaille? I suddenly have this irrepressible urge to know more.'

'Mais certainement!'

Chapter Three

'Madame, there is a telephone call for you, in the foyer,' Annette, the chambermaid announced, just as Rachel had reached a dramatic point in the book she was reading.

'Oh, Annette, be a dear, and take a message. Tell whoever it is that I'll ring back later. I am far too comfortable at the moment,' Rachel said suppressing a yawn and turning a page in the book.

'But Madame, it is a long distance call. And from a lady, I forget her name. Something like Mrs. Marrion?'

Rachel jumped up and said, 'Why didn't you say so earlier? That would be Mrs. Markham, my mother. I had better take her call or I'll never hear the end of it.'

Annette merely smiled and left the room, as Rachel dashed to the foyer and picked up the receiver, 'Hello Mums. How are you?'

She could hear a faint crackling sound as the voice on the other end came to life.

'Darling! I am fine. So sorry we missed your call the other day but I am glad that Betsy managed to get your hotel's name right,' Elizabeth Markham said, referring to their parlourmaid at Rutherford Hall.

'Betsy is a smart girl. She told me you and Dad had gone up to London.'

'Yes, your father and I had a meeting with one of those new fangled designers.'

'Why, what are you designing?'

'Oh, nothing really, just a new colour scheme, some new furniture and soft furnishings for our wing at Rutherford Hall. Our rooms are looking a tad tatty at the moment. And I wanted to spruce up everything before you and Jeremy got home. When are you getting home, by the way?'

'Hopefully in time for Christmas.'

'How lovely. And how is Paris? I hope the war hasn't completely ruined it.'

'Not really, Paris seems to have survived Herr Hitler's wrath, Mums. Although, by all accounts, our own Allied bombs caused far more damage over here.'

'Yes, darling, I remember reading somewhere that next to Germany, France was the most severely bomb-devastated country in this awful war!'

'You're right about that, Mums. Nevertheless, Paris is still beautiful and in the past couple of years they seem to have gotten back on their feet but it is a rather gloomy place, nothing like the bon vivant city of your description.'

'Oh dear, that was the roaring twenties, my darling when your father and I honeymooned in Paris. The gloriously lavish parties, the jazz and the excitement of it all. One can't expect the same level of gaiety anywhere, anymore. Ah! Those were the days. I'm afraid, the world has taken rather a gloomy turn since the great crash and subsequently the war.'

'I daresay, Mums. So, what new colour schemes have you chosen for the rooms?' Rachel asked, changing the subject to a brighter topic.

'Peacock blue for my boudoir, peach and ivory for the sitting room and your father insists on that horrid old racing green for his study but never mind that. I called to ask if you would do me a favour, while you're in Paris, darling.'

'Fire away, Mums. I was planning to do some Christmas shopping for you and Dad. Thought I'd get you a perfume this time. As you always say, a lady can never have too many fine French perfumes,' Rachel said with a smile.

'Oh, that would be lovely, darling. Chanel No. 5, or perhaps, Guerlain's Mitsouko would do very nicely! But that isn't quite what I called for. Darling, you do remember my old school friend, Prudence, don't you?'

'Er ...Mums, only from photographs and your reminisces. I don't quite have a personal memory of her, you know, considering I must have been about a year old when she last visited!'

'Of course, how silly of me. Well, around about the same time, twenty three years ago, shortly after she paid us that visit, she went and fell in love with that famous German concert pianist, Jonathan Rosenheim. She left her husband and ran away with Rosenheim to Munich. Her family was livid.'

'How interesting!'

'That's putting it mildly, my dear. In our days, it wasn't proper for married girls to run off with musicians, however talented they may have been.'

Rachel laughed out loud, 'I daresay! You make it sound like it's the done thing, these days!'

'Oh, well, these days nobody would bother to make such a fuss. They'd just label her a feisty young thing and get on with their own lives. Back then, her elopement sent shockwaves through society. To cut a long story short, as soon as her divorce came through, she married Rosenheim and had two children in prompt succession. We corresponded regularly and from her letters, I understood that she was deliriously happy and enjoyed her life in Germany immensely. But then the war came and the letters stopped. About a year ago, she wrote me once again. It seems they had a miserable time during the war – Oh Rachel, they were packed off to a concentration camp. Their son died there.'

'How awful.'

'Yes, it must have been ghastly. I can't even begin to imagine the things Pru must have had to endure. Anyhow she and her husband made it through the war and luckily, so did their daughter. I've forgotten the girl's name but from Pru's last letter, I understand that she is an artist and has her own studio. The family, rather, what's left of it, now live in Paris. I have the envelope in my hand and the return address reads as 127 Rue Saint Dominique, located in the 7th Arrondissement. I was wondering if you could look her up and take her a box of soft centred chocolates from me. As I recall, she used to love those.'

'It is sweet of you to remember, Mums. I'll throw in some flowers as well. And I promise I'll try calling her today to see if I can arrange a visit tomorrow. Do you have her telephone number?'

'No dear, I don't. But you could probably look up the Rosenheims at this address in the Parisian phone book. By all accounts, her husband is still quite famous.'

'I'll do that, Mums.'

'Thank you, darling. I'll trot along now. Give our love to Jeremy, dear and take care,' Elizabeth Markham said before she rang off.

II

Ten minutes later, Rachel had found the Rosenheim residence listed in the phone book and after what seemed like interminable number of rings, her call was finally answered by a man. His voice sounded cultured and Rachel instinctively realised that he was not a member of the household staff. She explained who she was and asked for Madame Rosenheim.

The man spoke in his soft genteel voice, 'I'm afraid, Madame, the Rosenheims are indisposed at the moment. If you would like to leave a message, I will be sure to pass on your condolences.'

'Condolences? I am sorry, Monsieur..., er, I did not get your name.'

'This is Aaron Berger. I am a friend of the family's. If you would like to attend the funeral, it is likely to be held the day after tomorrow at...'

'Sorry to interrupt, Monsieur Berger but,' Rachel faltered, 'I wasn't at all aware that there had been a death in the family.'

'I see. No, I should be the one to apologise. I presumed you heard of the tragedy which occurred this morning. Mademoiselle Isabelle is no longer with us. And naturally, her mother is inconsolable. '

'Yes, she must be. I am very sorry to hear about her loss. And yes, my husband and I would very much like to attend the funeral. Day after, did you say...'

'That is, if the Sûreté gives the go ahead. I am told there is to be an autopsy. It's all very distressing.'

'I am sure it is, Monsieur,' Rachel said and then, casting aside diplomacy, her curiosity piqued at the mention of the Sûreté, she asked, 'Was Isabelle's death accidental?'

His voice suddenly turned cold. 'I know nothing, Madame. All I have heard is that she was found lifeless at her studio in Montmartre this morning. Look, you are not a reporter, are you?' He asked with sudden alarm in his voice.

'Rest assured, Monsieur Berger. I too, am a friend of the family's, rather, my mother, Lady Elizabeth Markham, certainly is. You can check with Madame Rosenheim. I shan't take any more of your time but can you tell me if..' Rachel heard a click as the line went dead at the other end. Monsieur Berger must have panicked.

'...if I can visit her all the same. I would like to offer her my assistance,' Rachel trailed off as she put down the receiver, lost in thought.

Chapter Four

Inspector Beauchamp and Jeremy Richards were climbing a steep flight of stone stairs through a dusty and dark stairwell in an old building in Montmartre. In their quest to find Didier Lachaille – the man in charge of the Santinelli Case, the gendarme at the information desk at 'La Crim' had informed them that Lachaille had left the building and had given them an address in Montmartre, where he said the Inspector was likely to be found.

Beauchamp had located the street and building in Montmartre with ease and Jeremy was two steps behind him as they made their way up to the studio on the third floor. The wrought iron grating on the banisters was rusted and it was evident that the three story residential building was in decline. Varied smells visited their nostrils as they ascended, some pleasant – like a broth brewing on the first floor, and some not so pleasant, like the distinctive musty smell of a rather large family of rats in residence and their scattered droppings. As they reached the second floor landing, another pungent smell reached Jeremy's nose and obliterated all others. He could smell the sharp sting of turpentine along with a rancid metallic stench. Years of experience as a criminal investigator had taught him that this metallic stench could mean only one thing – copious amounts of spilt human blood.

From above, they could hear a man's voice giving authorative commands in a sharp staccato manner and then a figure in uniform descended towards the landing. In the dim light, Jeremy could see that it was a gendarme, a pale young man in his early twenties, with a handkerchief over his nose. He was heaving, as if to control the urge to retch. His eyes bore a haunted look that Jeremy knew so well and had seen before at crime scenes especially amongst new recruits. He also knew that their souls would harden up as time went by and eventually that puzzled haunted look would give way to another – a look of déjà vu, the sad knowledge that these eyes had seen it all before.

Inspector Beauchamp said something in rapid French and the boy answered. Jeremy could not make out exactly what had been said but vaguely understood that their talk was about sending someone downstairs.

Jeremy asked quietly, 'Henri, would you like me to go downstairs and wait for you?'

'Non, non. Allez. We must go up. This gendarme is being sent down to make sure that no one else can come up.'

The scene that greeted them on the top floor was fantastic. The narrowness of the stairwell and the small, insignificant door leading into the studio had not prepared Jeremy for the vastness of the space that he had stepped into. A huge skylight in the center of the ceiling along with four large windows in the west, allowed the silver light from the pale Sun into its vast proportions. Canvasses in varying sizes were stacked along the eastern wall. A large easel, holding an eight by ten canvas stood sideways, in the center of the room. It had the effect of dividing the large luminous hall into two. Tubs of paints, turpentine, palette knives and brushes were scattered on the floor and atop a rustic wooden table in front of the canvas.

Whatever activity was going on, was evidently on the other side of the canvas, from where the staccato commands were ensuing. As Beauchamp made his way to the other side, Jeremy followed keeping a discreet distance. The last thing he wanted, was to get off on the wrong foot with Didier Lachaille. There were three men in the room.

Beauchamp hollered, 'Allo, Didier. Ce qui se passe?'

The man in question looked up. He had curly ginger hair, large green eyes, set close together and a bushy moustache that gave his large square head some sense of proportion. He had thickset shoulders and a stocky torso.

Didier had been kneeling over what looked like a human body, which was being covered in a tarpaulin, ready to be moved for further medical examination. He grunted at Beauchamp before rising to his full height of about five feet, two inches. As the man stood up, Jeremy had the strange notion that the length of his short bandy legs equalled that of his torso. He had seen people like this in London's music halls. The kind of people who came in as comic relief between two acts. But that is where the resemblance ended. This man had a commanding aura, which was unmistakable. A little Napoleon alright, thought Jeremy, as Didier tiptoed around the pools of congealed, dark blood and reached Beauchamp. The two men spoke in French and Didier nodded in acknowledgement at Jeremy.

'Very pleased to meet you, Inspector Lachaille,' Jeremy said as he stepped forward to shake his hand. 'Extremely sorry to intrude upon your investigation like this.'

Lachaille looked up at him and said in an even voice, 'Non. We are almost finished here. The landlady called us in. She found this woman, the artist, lying here with her throat slit when she came to clean this morning. My team has already collected all the evidence.'

Beauchamp spoke, 'That sounds familiar.'

Lachaille added, 'Yes. A second murder in a Montmartre art studio. Yet another victim found with a slit throat. This doesn't look good.'

'Do you think there may be a connection with the Santinelli murder?' Jeremy ventured carefully.

'We'll see, 'Lachaille answered with an even gaze directed at Jeremy.

'Who's the victim? Have you managed to contact the next of kin?' Beauchamp asked.

'Oui, the victim's name is Isabelle Rosenheim.' He glanced at his notepad and continued, 'Her father came in some time back. A Jonathan Rosenheim. I tried to stop him but he insisted on seeing the body.'

'Non! She is not *the* Jonathan Rosenheim's daughter?' Beauchamp asked with some trepidation.

'Oui. The same,' Lachaille responded.

'Merde!'

'Why, what's the matter?' Jeremy asked.

'He is a tres, tres famous musician. Ca va chiér!'

'Sorry?' Jeremy asked uncomprehendingly.

Beauchamp explained. 'As you English say, now the shit is really going to hit the fan!'

Didier responded calmly, 'That is as may be. We will get our man now. I was waiting for the murderer to show his hand. This one is pompous but intelligent. He will, as we say, trip on his cleverness and fall into my net.'

'So you have connected the two murders,' Jeremy said with a smile.

'But then why did you arrest Dubois' mistress?' Beauchamp asked.

He replied with a smug smile, 'I had to bait him into believing we are *fier imbeciles...* prize idiots. That is the only way to trap a man like him.'

'I will be honest. I don't understand your methods, Didier,' Beauchamp said, shaking his head.

'Come, there is a cafe two doors away. We'll get some coffee and croissants, I haven't had lunch,' Didier said calmly as he steered them towards the door. And Jeremy had a hunch that he was in the presence of an extraordinary mind.

Chapter Five

The next afternoon Rachel and Jeremy joined Count Santinelli for luncheon in the private dining room at The Ritz. For the first time in days, the clouds had parted to give way to a golden sunlight that slanted in through the sheer curtains of the gilded room and glinted back from the silverware and glasses on the immaculately laid table.

The Count smiled as he said, 'I am glad that you have decided to take on this case. Now I can rest easy that Pietro will not go unpunished.'

'You seem very sure that it was him. What if we find out it wasn't him?' Jeremy asked with a raised eyebrow.

The Count shrugged. 'If you can give me proof of his innocence, we'll see. For now I want you to concentrate on getting proof of his guilt.' Then he turned and beckoned the waiter, who was hovering discreetly in the background, 'Versez le champagne, s'il vous plait.'

As the waiter took the bottle out of the ice bucket and poured champagne in their flutes, the Count raised a toast, 'To justice, for Sarah.'

Rachel raised her flute in acknowledgment and took a sip. She relaxed deeper into the fauteuil as champagne bubbles sparkled on the roof of her mouth like sunshine reflected on water. Suddenly it struck her as she glanced around the elegant room that the three of them sat suspended in golden light. It gave her a strange sensation of sudden and intense well being and the awareness that life was good, despite all the chaos and disarray caused by human activity in this world. In moments like this, it was easy to see the fullness and perfection of it all.

She was brought out of her reverie as Jeremy addressed her, 'Don't you agree, darling?'

'I'm sorry, I was lost in thought. What were you saying?' She responded with a smile.

'I was just expressing my belief that the French truly know how to live. The Count has just informed us that we are about to experience authentic French cuisine - a seven course, cordon bleu menu, no less.'

'How marvellous!'

The Count spoke up, 'But I want to add that when it comes to love of good food and wine, we Italians are not far behind.'

Rachel responded, 'Oh, I know. I spent a year in Florence studying Renaissance art. But I was only sixteen back then and mother wouldn't allow me more than a few sips of Chianti once every now and then. But I would really love to visit Italy someday with Jeremy.'

'If you both ever come to Italy, I will show you the countryside near my ancestral villa in Campania. From there you can see green terraces sloping down towards the Tyrrhenian Sea. My villa is surrounded by olive gardens and citrus orchards. Ah, the aromas of oranges, lemons and orange blossoms, it fills the air. It is so beautiful. We have a vineyard as well, but to be honest, the wine from it, is undrinkable,' he said with a boyish grin.

'Don't you miss Italy?' Rachel asked as the first course was served.

'I do, of course but during the war, I was exiled from my homeland. After the war ended, it has been one thing after another and now I consider Paris my home. Also I am fearful of what I will find if I do go back to Italy now.'

'Why were you exiled?' Rachel asked.

'The war changed my country so much. In the early years, Mussolini and his fascists made life impossible for us. They executed my elder brother who was openly against Mussolini signing Hitler's Manifesto of Race. They came after me too. I had no choice but to flee overnight. It's a long and tiresome story. All I will say is that during the war, I joined the Resistance and I have been in France ever since.'

'What about Pietro?'

'He fancied he was a fascist until he joined them and saw firsthand what that really meant. Then he switched sides and begged me to help him escape their clutches.'

'And you did?'

'Yes, I did. I was in touch with undercover members of the Resistance there and I asked them to help. But now I wish I hadn't.'

Rachel spoke. 'I need to ask you why you feel this way about your own brother if he realized his mistake in joining the fascists. I am sure he must've been very young at the time.'

'He was old enough to know that they were cold blooded killers and he still went with them. He is unstable and he is still under the malicious influence of certain people here in Paris. I feel it in my bones that he is not entirely unsympathetic towards the fascist ideal. You should know that even today there are undercover fascist cells operating all over Europe, even here in Paris.'

Jeremy spoke. 'But surely you don't suspect that your wife's murder is linked to them?'

'I don't know what I suspect. You see, I have known for some time now that he was taking large sums of money from her.'

'Do you know why she was giving him money?' Rachel queried.

'I asked but she said that he was helping her with some investments.'

'And you don't believe that?'

'I don't believe for a moment that Pietro knew anything about finance or investments.'

'Did you question him?'

'Of course but he claimed that the money was for an art dealer, who had some old masters to sell. For a while, I believed him. I knew that it amused Sarah to think that she was an art aficionado. Of late, she had been visiting art exhibits and picking up pieces of art for the new home we were in the process of decorating.'

'So what changed your mind?'

'The fact that she was killed in his friend's studio and I have a feeling that she had found out something that he did not want known!'

'Wait a minute! Alexandre Dubois was Pietro's friend?'

'Yes, it was Pietro who put her onto this nonsense of getting her portrait painted by Dubois for the Hall in the new house. Something on the lines of a modern version of Botticelli. Dubois is famous for copying Botticelli's stroke.'

'But what would be Pietro's motive for murdering her?'

'I think that maybe she began suspecting that his masters were not so old. The night before she was killed, I heard them having words. Rather, she was shouting and he was mumbling. I was outside the door and I think the argument was over a Rembrandt that his friend was supposed to procure for her.'

'Do you suspect that Pietro is involved in a forgery ring?'

'It could be but I can't be sure. You see when I entered the room, they both went quiet and Sarah made some excuse and left. Pietro too said he had to meet some friends and walked out. If he is involved in some criminal activity that is linked to Sarah's death, I want to know. And that is what I want you to find out.'

'Yes, we will. By the way, did your wife make a will?'

'No, she was so young. I am sure the thought never crossed her mind.'

'But surely, being a recipient of such a vast inheritance, she would have been advised to?' Rachel asked.

'Of course but you didn't know Sarah. She was so alive. And she never really paid attention to all those legal advisors from England. She avoided them like the plague especially after we got married.'

Jeremy spoke, 'So you inherit everything as next of kin?'

'Yes but if you are thinking...'

Jeremy explained, 'No, it isn't that. I already know that you could not have killed your wife. I have some friends in the Sûreté and they were kind enough to share some of the case history with me. As you must know that in a murder investigation of this sort, the spouse is always the first suspect and the police have categorically ruled you out based on your watertight alibi.'

'So what is it, then?'

'Just an unkind thought; that if anything were to happen to you, Pietro would inherit both the title and your wealth.'

'Rest assured that I am not going to be as easy to murder as my wife was,' he said, as he unbuttoned his waistcoat to reveal the holster strapped to his chest. 'This is a very reliable weapon. Besides, I am already on my guard.'

'That's a relief. However this is just conjecture. It may not have been Pietro. He did have an alibi as well, you know.'

'Pietro's alibi is based on the word of one friend. He claims that they walked from Aaron's house, and went all the way up to the terraced gardens of the Sacré-Cœur on a cold and dark evening, which I find hard to believe and no one else can corroborate the story other than this one lady who may have somehow been coerced into giving him an alibi.'

'I will need to find out more. Do you know her name?'

'Yes, her family is known to me. She is an artist – Isabelle Rosenheim.'

Jeremy gasped and said out loud, 'My God! That's why Didier was so smug when he spoke about the killer finally falling into his trap.'

'What was that?' The Count asked.

Jeremy responded, 'There may be something in that theory of yours, after all. They are trying to keep it under wraps for a few more hours until the report from the medical examiner gets in, but it will be in the morning edition of all newspapers, so I may as well tell you now. Isabelle Rosenheim was found murdered in her studio yesterday. What's more, she may have been murdered by the same person who killed your wife. She was also found with her throat slit.'

'I don't believe it. How do you know about this?' The Count looked perplexed.

Jeremy answered, 'I was there in her studio, just a few hours after they found her body. I had gone with an old friend from the Sûreté to meet Inspector Lachaille who, as you know, is also in charge of your wife's case.'

'I see!'

'Just one more question. Do you know the name of the friend who was supposedly sourcing the Rembrandt for your wife?' Jeremy asked.

'Yes, I heard Pietro mention a well known art dealer in Montmartre. His name is Aaron Berger.'

It was Rachel's turn to gasp.

Chapter Six

The next day dawned bright and though it was colder than the day before, the Sun played hide and seek with the clouds that floated leisurely across the Parisian sky. After they had breakfasted, Jeremy had gone out to meet Inspector Beauchamp. Rachel knew she had to be outside on a day like this and she made up her mind to pay the Rosenheims a visit. She placed a call to the Rosenheim residence, which was answered by their butler, who informed her that Madame was home and that the funeral was to be held the day after.

After giving it some thought, she chose not to dress in black. After all, she had never met Isabelle Rosenheim and to her mind it seemed as though wearing black would be an exaggerated display of mourning for someone she did not know. Instead, she chose to wear her simple yet stylish new coffee brown sheath dress with a matching coat and paired her outfit with brown suede Mary Janes, which she had recently picked up at a boutique on the Champs-Elysees. Only in Paris, could you find shoes that combined style and comfort with such panache. As a final touch, she dabbed Chanel No. 5 on her pulse points. She smiled as she remembered Coco Chanel's famous quote that her mother often repeated to her through her growing years – *'Perfume is the unseen, unforgettable, ultimate accessory of fashion that heralds your arrival and prolongs your departure.'* Her toilette complete, she observed herself in the mirror, adjusted her cloche and felt satisfied with the way she looked. She headed downstairs and left a note for Jeremy before stepping out to make her way to the Left Bank.

Rue Saint Dominique was a picturesque street. Walking through it, Rachel had the strange sensation that the Eiffel Tower was looming over her, larger than life, watching her every move, like an inert iron monster that could spring to life at any moment. She stopped to observe it for a moment. It dominated the sky view from where she stood. The street itself was charming. It was flanked on either side by elegant apartment buildings, which had large French windows overlooking the street through intricately designed wrought iron railings.

She resumed walking and walked past a book shop and patisserie that emanated the aroma of freshly baked bread. Just across the street there was another cafe. She spotted a florist shop next to it and crossed the street to buy some flowers for Mrs. Rosenheim.

The entrance to 127 was through a wrought iron gate that led into a small lobby. Rachel could see the interior courtyard from where she stood. The apartments were wrapped around this central open space and it gave the windows facing the courtyard, a view of the large abstract marble sculpture placed on a block of stone, which stood at the center of the courtyard. The sculpture was surrounded by flowering stone urns and a profusion of greenery. Stone benches were placed strategically around the courtyard. It looked like a restful place. She spoke with the building concierge, who guided her to take the elevator up to the second floor.

Rachel rang the doorbell and was let in shortly by the Rosenheim's butler. He took her card and showed her into a midsized sitting room. She noticed that the decor comprised of a mixture of baroque and Japanese influences. Colour, glass, mirrors and light dominated the room; the furnishings were bright and cream tulle curtains hung at the large French windows that overlooked the street, she had just been walking on. She walked over to the window to admire the view from the second floor.

The door reopened and a tall, elegant, middle aged lady walked in. She had dark hair swept up into a French knot and was dressed in a simple black dress with pearls around her throat. Rachel recognised her from her mother's photographs. She was older, of course, her face was lined and her eyes wore signs of grief but there was no mistake that this was Prudence Rosenheim. Rachel walked over to her and said, 'Good morning, Mrs. Rosenheim. I know this isn't the best time to visit you but I'm Elizabeth Markham's daughter, Rachel. I am in Paris for a few weeks and Mummy absolutely insisted that I pay you a visit. I had called earlier.'

Prudence smiled and said softly and slowly in a lilting voice, 'Of course, you are Elizabeth's daughter. The resemblance is striking. And you've brought flowers. How kind. Come, let me look at you, my dear. The last time I saw you, you had just learnt how to walk. Yes the same face, but now you look so elegant, just like your mother used to, when we were young.'

'She remembers you well and she asked me to bring you soft centered chocolates but I thought that under the circumstances...'

'You've heard then.'

'Yes. I can't begin to tell you how sorry I am, Mrs. Rosenheim.'

'Yes. I can't quite believe it myself. The past forty eight hours have been like reliving an old nightmare. You see, I lost my son, Joel, four years ago,' she said, as unbidden tears started flowing down her cheeks.

'Yes, Mummy told me briefly what you went through during the war.'

'We couldn't even say goodbye or give him a decent burial. He was such a gentle boy. And those animals - they just shot him in cold blood in front of our eyes and flung him in a heap with the others, into a pit in the ground. I saw them shovel dirt over my boy.' She dabbed her eyes with a handkerchief. 'If a mother can survive a thing like that, one assumes you can survive anything. But I never dreamt my Isabelle would be killed just as ruthlessly in a civilised place as Paris,' she wept, as Rachel put her arm around her shoulder and guided her to the sofa.

Mrs. Rosenheim sat down and took a few moments to compose herself. 'I am sorry, Rachel, I don't know what's come over me. I have forgotten my manners. Please, won't you sit down?'

Rachel thought of saying, 'I know how difficult this must be for you,' but even to her own ears it sounded so lame. She found herself thinking, 'If only there was something I could do or say, to make it better,' but what could anyone possibly do or say to a mother who has lost both her children in such brutal ways. So she sat down and remained silent.

Her eyes went to a large photograph on the mantelpiece. It was a beautiful black and white photograph of the Rosenheim family that must have been taken over a decade ago. A young Jonathan Rosenheim was seated at the grand piano, in a luxuriously appointed drawing room, smiling up at the camera, while Prudence stood just behind him, looking beautiful in a full length white lace tea gown. She had one hand on her husband's shoulder and a contented smile upon her lips that managed to convey happiness, love and pride simultaneously. In the foreground, two young children - a boy and a girl were seated on a Persian carpet. The boy was smiling up at the camera while the little girl looked upon her older brother with open adulation. There was something wonderful and natural about the way the photographer had captured a happy moment for this family. It was an unusual picture taken by a gifted photographer. Merely observing it gave Rachel a catch in her throat.

Prudence spoke quietly as she observed Rachel's expression. 'Yes, I look at that photograph and I feel the same way. It was taken only fourteen years ago but it seems like a picture from another lifetime now.'

'Was that taken in your house in Germany?'

Prudence spoke with a voice that was reviving the ghosts. 'Yes. We were so happy back then. It was a golden time for both of us. Jonathan's concert appearances were being applauded by music critics across the world and I had my beautiful home and children. A photographer from Life magazine – Mark Hammond came all the way from America to take our pictures. He told us he wanted to capture the maestro in his home and give the world a glimpse of him as a family man.'

'Your home must have been very beautiful. That room alone looks so inviting.'

'Yes, the house had been in Jonathan's family for generations. It was a treasure trove of antiques and beautiful handmade pieces of furniture. It was magnificent. Even the fountains and sculptures in the garden were late 18th

century. Now that lone photograph is our only reminder that we ever lived there. In one fell stroke it was all taken away from us. When the Gestapo finally came to take us away, all we could take with us were a few sets of clothes to protect us from the bitter cold. They gave us exactly five minutes to pack and watched over us like hawks while we did. We were not allowed to take anything but a suitcase of clothes. Even that photograph you see was left behind. I wrote to Mark Hammond much later, after we came to Paris and he very kindly sent me another print.'

'Why didn't you leave Germany when the others did? Before the darkness. We heard that so many people chose to sell their homes and leave with their belongings, for safer shores just before it all began.'

'I pleaded with Jonathan when our neighbours, the Lichtensteins sold their home and left for America but he was so sure that all that talk of impending doom for Jews was exaggerated nonsense propagated by a bunch of pessimistic nihilists. The house was his ancestral home, as was Germany and he was so passionate about staying on. He said that no one could ask us to leave. After all Germany was one of the most civilised countries in Europe – culturally, socially and historically. And if some trouble did come upon the Jews, he insisted that come what may, no harm would come to us, our family would be safe. He was a famous man and he knew people high up in the government. And sadly we both lived by that fairytale and stayed on till the day they came to cart us off to Dachau – the concentration camp. If only we had left when the Lichtensteins did, my Joel would still be alive and we would still have some of our beloved things that made our house a home. But bad decisions are always so clearly bad, only in retrospect. At the time we make them they seem like sensible choices.'

They sat quietly for a while mulling over all that had been experienced and shared then Prudence broke the silence between them. 'Come, let us talk about something else. Tell me, how is your mother?'

'She is fine and she talks about you often. I know that she would have liked to be here to comfort you.'

'Your mother has always been a comfort to me. She is the only friend I have kept in touch with since I left England. You may not know this but she stood by me when it seemed that the rest of the world, including my family, shunned me and I will always remember her kindness.'

'You both were very close as girls, weren't you?'

'We were friends, yes, we were at school together and your mother was quite popular but I never discovered what amazing strength of character she had, until much later, until I was about to leave England. Life is strange that way. It is only when one faces difficult times that one realises who one's true friends are. Your mother has been that kind of a rare friend to me. I remember it surprised me at the time. She was the only one, amongst the many people I had known all my life, who came to visit me often. She always brought me soft centered chocolates. I had no money – my family had cut me off when I moved in with Jonathan. One day she came and took me shopping to Harrods and bought me a beautiful new dress and hat. She told me that I couldn't marry Jonathan in an old dress and that it was her wedding gift to me. No one else in the world would have thought of doing something like that other than a woman who could put herself in someone else's shoes, and think of what that person really needed. I have received many gifts from kind friends over the years but that one gesture of your mother's touched my heart beyond all others.'

Rachel smiled at her reminisces but said nothing. She was overwhelmed with pride at being her mother's daughter. She had always loved her mother but miles away from home, hearing a stranger speak about her kindness, made her see her mother in a new light, with a renewed sense of awe and respect.

'Thank you for sharing this with me, Mrs. Rosenheim.'

'Please, call me Prudence.'

Rachel said with a smile, 'Yes, I will. Now it is my turn to share something with you, Prudence. I have a confession to make.'

'Yes?'

'The thing is, that neither mother nor I knew anything about this tragic event in your family, when she called me the day before yesterday and asked me to visit you. But since then, as you mentioned earlier, life is strange indeed and my husband and I are caught up in investigating a case that may be closely linked with what happened to your daughter, Isabelle.'

'Investigating a case? I don't understand, my dear.'

'I think I had better explain.' Rachel said and proceeded to tell her about Jeremy's past career at Scotland Yard, their involvement in solving prior murder cases and their current assignment with the Santinelli case. She continued, 'So, you see. It was almost like serendipity when Jeremy informed me that the two crimes may be related. And since we are already investigating the first, I would like you to know that we will leave no stone unturned to catch the culprit responsible for Isabelle's death.'

When Rachel had finished, they heard the door bell chime in the distance. Prudence leaned forward and took her hand. In her quiet way she began to speak. 'I see. All that you have told me is very impressive, really it is. But before we are interrupted, I must tell you something. When you have lived as long as I have and seen the things I have, you will understand when I tell you that this is a ruthless world and I would not want you or your husband to take any unnecessary risks for our sake. The living must go on living. You are young with your whole life ahead of you. Take my advice – the advice of a weary old woman who has seen too much and go back to England. Go home. No good can ever come of this.'

At the very moment that she finished speaking, as she had prophesied, they were interrupted. The door opened and the Butler entered the room. He addressed Prudence, 'Monsieur Berger est arrivé, Madame.'

She let go of Rachel's hand and sat upright. 'Merci. Please, show him in.'

Chapter Seven

On the other side of town, a cell door was clanked open and the gendarme announced, 'Suzette Bouvier.'

There were eight women in the holding cell. Most were in various stages of inebriation and disarray. A smell of stale perfume and urine pervaded the dark, dreary space.

One small mouse like woman got up from the far end of the worn and scratched wooden bench and made her way towards the gendarme. She was dressed conservatively and walked with her head bowed.

As she passed by, there was a raucous cheer from two cell mates, who were obviously there because of their suspected ties to the oldest profession in the world.

One told the other in French that she wished *she* had a lover who would bail her out, like this lucky mouse and the other one spat in derision and replied that if all one needed was a lover, she would have been out of this rotten hell hole in ten seconds of being bunged in there. Her friend shook her head and informed her that with the right connections, it didn't matter even if you were in for murder, like the mouse. And that a lover with connections is what they both needed. And her friend threw her head back and laughed. She managed to splutter in between her guffaws that she'd be sure to ask for that, come Christmas.

Suzette heard their jibes but did not look at them. Her hand was on the little silver pendant at her bosom, which held the picture of Mother Mary holding baby Jesus.

She was escorted through a dingy passageway, up two flights of stairs and shown into the administrative wing. The main hall was scattered with desks manned by half a dozen or so administrators, whose job was to get the paperwork in order for charge sheets.

She was guided to a desk on the right where she saw three men seated. Jeremy was among them. The only one she recognised was Inspector Lachaille.

Didier Lachaille spoke and told her something in French, which Jeremy understood as, 'You are free to go, Mademoiselle.'

'Free to go? Just like that?' She responded in French.

'Yes, we made a mistake. I apologise. The murderer struck again.'

'Oh!' She cried with a fleeting look of horror and then her eyes took on a puzzled look but she said nothing more.

'You can sign these release forms, and take your things from the desk over there,' Lachaille instructed her.

She nodded and bent over to sign the papers that were pushed in front of her. Then without a word she walked away to collect her things.

Didier turned to Jeremy and said, 'She knows something. What, I do not know but she is hiding something. I can feel it.'

Jeremy responded, 'Didier, if you don't mind my saying so, why don't you have her followed?'

'I would, if I had enough men. It's the war. Not enough men left.'

'Perhaps I can help. With your permission, of course.'

'You'll probably get lost, or worse get robbed. You don't know your way around Paris.'

'Don't worry about me. My French is passable. I'll manage. So, what do you say?'

Didier shrugged, 'If you wish. Anyhow, she's probably going to head back to Dubois' studio.'

II

Jeremy shadowed her at a safe distance. Suzette turned on the main street and he realised that she was headed in the opposite direction from Montmartre. She was carrying a worn old satchel. She walked for about three blocks and entered a pawn shop.

Jeremy bought a newspaper and a packet of cigarettes from the tobacconist next door and lit one. He could see through the stained window panes of the shop. She was talking to the potbellied owner and handed over some money to him. He went to the back through the door behind the counter and came out with a large package wrapped in brown paper, tied up with strings. She opened it and to Jeremy's surprise, it was a large wooden model airplane. She looked at it and then wrapped up the package again. As she made her way towards the door, carrying the bulky package, he quickly stubbed out his cigarette and got ready to follow her once more.

She then started walking towards Pont Marie Metro station. Five minutes later she was at the ticket window and purchased a fare to Gare de l'Est. Jeremy followed suit. He had a vague idea that she was headed for the suburbs. A few minutes later, the train pulled onto the platform and she boarded. He followed and sat two rows behind her as the train pulled out of the station again. Jeremy read the French newspaper for a while, as the train made its way to Gare de l'Est. About twenty minutes later, she alighted from the metro and walked towards the Gare de l'Est railway station. It was about two minutes walking distance. Once inside she walked towards the left-luggage lockers and gave the attendant a ticket from her satchel. Moments later, she collected a dark brown medium size Gladstone bag. Jeremy saw her rummage through her satchel to bring out a small bronze key. She then went to a corner and opened the Gladstone to look inside. Apparently satisfied that the contents were still in their place, she closed it and locked it once again.

She then hung the satchel diagonally across her shoulder, tucked the model airplane under her left arm and held the Gladstone with her right and walked over to the ticket counter. At the counter, Jeremy heard her ask for a one-way fare to Bobigny. Jeremy stayed close behind and bought his fare. Once they boarded the train he found a window seat a few rows in front of her. Ten minutes into the journey, he set down the paper he was reading and looked out the window. They were passing through a grimy industrial zone with tall brick chimneys. The factories belched out thick black smoke into the grey clouds overhead. The journey became slightly more scenic only once they moved past the industrial suburb. Three stops later, he glanced back and saw her get up and collect her things as the train slowed down once again. She passed by his seat and he waited for a few more passengers to get off before disembarking.

The Sun had come out from behind the clouds once again as he followed her through the streets. She walked for another fifteen minutes through lanes and bylanes that had small rundown two story row houses with a patch of garden in front. She stopped at a wooden gate in front of a dilapidated row house, which looked like it could have used a lick of paint. Jeremy noticed a small boy of about five playing in the garden patch. The little boy looked up as the gate creaked open and his tiny face lit up with an ecstatic smile as he came running towards her, shouting in French, 'Maman! Maman! You've come. I knew you would.'

She set down her Gladstone and the large brown package and went down on her knees as he came into her arms. She held the little boy and kissed him vigorously as he put his scrawny arms around her neck and hugged her back. Jeremy couldn't help but stop and smile at them. The boy who was facing him looked up with curious eyes and Jeremy heard him ask in French, 'Maman, who's that man?'

As she turned to look at him, Jeremy fancied he saw a fleeting glint of recognition in her eyes and then it was gone. He tipped his hat at them and walked on casually. He could hear her tell her son in French, 'Nobody, just a man on the street. Here, look what I've brought for you, my darling.'

Chapter Eight

Meanwhile, back in the Rosenheim's apartment, a flamboyantly dressed man in his early forties was shown into the sitting room. He was good-looking, trim, about 5'10", with a straight nose, penetrating eyes, salt and pepper hair and a goatee that gave his face a distinctive look. Had she seen him at a party, Rachel would have assumed him to be a diplomat of some standing, perhaps even an ambassador. He had that distinctive appearance of a man who is aware of his own importance and place in this world. When he spoke, his pleasing baritone voice matched his appearance, 'Ma cherie, je suis désolé. I did not know you had a visitor. I can come back later, yes? I would not like to interrupt your tête-à-tête.'

'Not at all, Aaron. Do come in and meet my charming guest. Rachel, this is Aaron Berger, a dear friend and Aaron, this lovely girl is visiting from England. She is my friend, Elizabeth Markham's daughter – Rachel.'

'Enchanté, Mademoiselle,' he said kissing her proffered hand and holding it for a few seconds longer than necessary.

Rachel smiled as she reclaimed her hand and said, 'It is Madame, and I have had the pleasure of your acquaintance already, Monsieur. We spoke over the telephone the day before.'

'Ah, je suis tres désolé! I did not realise, I was speaking with such a beautiful lady. You must think me very rude. Please forgive my insolence,' Berger replied dramatically.

Rachel responded, 'Please, don't mention it. It was my fault. I called at a difficult time. At any rate, I am glad I have a better effect in person than I do over the telephone.' She turned to Prudence and explained with a smile, 'He mistook me for a reporter when I first called.'

Before Prudence could say anything, Berger spoke, 'Madame, you must allow me to make amends. I would like to invite you out to lunch with us, if you are free.'

Rachel responded, 'That is very kind, Monsieur Berger but I know how busy you all must be at a time like this and I should not like to be in the way.'

'However busy one is, one has to eat, yes? You must join us. We have some funeral arrangements to see to and then we get something to eat.' Turning to Prudence, he said, 'Are you ready, ma cherie?'

'I am sorry Aaron. I forgot to tell you that I cannot go. You will have to help with the flowers and selecting the casket.'

'Why, what's happened?'

'Jonathan just telephoned to say that he is on his way back and we have to go back to meet the Inspector. Both of us need to sign some documents before we can get Isabelle away from the police morgue. Rachel, I know it is a terrible thing to ask of you but it would be very kind if you could accompany Aaron and help him...'

'Not at all. It's the least I can do. It will be my privilege to help in any way I can.' Turning to Berger she said, 'Shall we go, Monsieur?'

II

They spent the better part of the morning selecting the right casket and the flowers for the funeral. There was something strangely intimate about two strangers carrying out these tasks together. Death had the power to temporarily submerge social protocols and accelerate human bonding. By the time they had finished, they were on a first name basis.

Rachel spoke philosophically as they exited the funeral home, 'If this experience has taught me anything, Aaron, it is that life is short and we must make what we can out of it before it is gone.'

Aaron responded, 'I don't believe life is short at all. It is a lie propagated by pessimists. Don't allow such thoughts to enter your head, ma cherie. Tell me, what else in your life's experience has been longer than your life itself? Life, when you live it to the fullest, with joy for every moment, is the longest thing there is. And I guarantee you that your life is the single longest thing you will personally experience on this Earth.'

'I'll say, that is true. Quite a different perspective from what one hears normally.'

'When I was a boy, I taught myself never to be ordinary and follow beliefs blindly. I didn't want to be like the others. Like cattle. So, I question everything, even the simplest things. For example right now the question running in my head is, are you hungry? And I hope that you are, ma cherie,' Berger said with a twinkle in his eye.

'Absolutely famished, Aaron. I could eat a horse,' she replied, as she walked down the stone steps with her arm linked through his.

'I am glad to hear it. We will treat ourselves to a grand luncheon and rest our weary souls. Death can be a tiring business for those who are left behind.'

'Yes, I suppose it can. So, where are we going?' She asked, as Berger's chauffeur brought the car around.

'To Maxim's, of course. The only place in Paris where one can replenish both the body and soul. The food is, ah, très bonne, and the wine, sublime,' he said, as he opened the car door for her.

'Oh! But I am not dressed for Maxim's!'

'Nonsense! You are a very beautiful young lady. Moreover, I like your style – simple and elegant. And it's a good thing you're not all flounce and frills. Did you hear about the Dior fiasco in Paris, earlier this year?'

'No... I mean yes. Everyone knows Dior stormed the fashion world with his 'Corolle' show in February. It was in every magazine one could get one's hands on, if that's what you mean. I'd hardly call that a fiasco! More like a thumping success, wouldn't you say?'

'No, ma cherie, I am talking about the *fiasco* that ensued later at Montmartre, where they were doing a photography session of that very same line of fashion.'

'No. What happened?'

'One moment, excusez-moi,' he said, as he gave instructions to the chauffeur to drive them to Maxim's. Then turning to Rachel he explained, 'In the middle of that photo shoot, the Dior models were attacked by the impoverished women vendors of Montmartre. I heard they tore viciously at the beautiful dresses leaving the models half naked on the street.'

'How awful! Why on Earth did they do that?' She asked, as the chauffeur manoeuvred the car on to the main road.

'Ma cherie, his timing was terrible – bordering on insensitive. Paris was just coming out of uniforms. There was war time austerity everywhere and here this man goes and designs dresses that need 25 yards of the finest material money can buy.'

'Twenty five yards for a single dress! I daresay I'm no longer surprised that they were attacked! While I personally don't care for those wasp waists and huge flouncy skirts he makes, in England we still can't get our hands on more than 3 yards of good material at a time, for love or money. Material is still rationed, you know.'

'As it was, over here. Thankfully things are a little better now.'

'Which is why, I devoted my first week in Paris to get my wardrobe in order. But that Dior story will certainly make for interesting dinner conversation back home. Though I can't help but feel rather sorry for the models. It wasn't really their fault.'

'Yes, my dear. But I must confess that as a man, I would've given anything to have witnessed the cat fight.' He said with a wink in her direction. 'Such a pity I missed it. And right in the middle of my neck of the woods too!'

'You live in Montmartre? How interesting. I've only visited the Sacre-Coeur so far. But I did read in my Baedeker that Vincent Van Gogh, Toulouse-Lautrec and Émile Bernard lived and worked there. Is that true? Or is that just something tourists like to hear?'

'No. It's true, hundreds of artists lived in Montmartre, over the past century and many of them turned out to be quite famous. It used to be a village really. But what your guide book may not tell you, is that the majority of them lived on what Van Gogh described as the *petits boulevard,* closer to the butte, or the top of the hill. As you go up the roads get narrower and the rents get cheaper.'

'And is your house there, as well?'

'Heavens, no! While the butte is a perfectly charming place to visit, you couldn't possibly live there. It's a tad on the rough side. You'll find all kinds of people there – artists, musicians, writers, revolutionaries. Apart from that it's mostly a gritty, working class neighbourhood.'

'So, where do you live, Aaron?'

'I live on the lower slopes, on Rue de L'Abreuvoir, to be precise. Just two doors down from Château des Brouillards – Renoir's old house. He lived there in the 1880s.'

'How fascinating and did Van Gogh have a name for your street too?'

'As a matter of fact, he did – he called it the grands boulevard.'

'That does sound rather grand!'

'It is, even if I say so myself. I consider myself lucky to have found a house there. It has a beautiful garden. A peaceful haven, far from the maddening noise and gaiety of Paris. My art galerie is also close by. You should come and see it for yourself.'

'I'd love to. But you know something? I'd have thought that a man-about-town like you would have preferred a townhouse or an apartment in the heart of town.'

'Well, I have that too. You were there this morning.'

'The Rosenheim's apartment belongs to you?'

'Yes.'

'So you rent it out to them?'

'No, do I look like a rent collector to you?'

'No. You don't.' Rachel laughed. 'So you just let them live there?'

'What else can I do? I met Jonathan a year ago and found out that he was living in a sordid hotel, en famille. And I found myself thinking it was sacrilege that a great man – a great pianist like him should be brought down to living like that just because a few pig-headed nations can't see eye to eye.'

'But I should have thought that a famous musician like him would be earning enough to own a decent place of his own.'

'In a perfect world, yes. But not in this one. Artists and musicians – even famous ones don't earn what they deserve, ma cherie. Besides, what do you expect, the Nazis took away everything they had. *Every last Reichspfennig.* They came to Paris with nothing. He started from scratch only a year and a half ago.'

Rachel smiled at him and then leaned over to kiss his cheek. 'You are a kind man, Aaron. And a good man. And I am so glad that I got a chance to get to know you better.'

Chapter Nine

The Rosenheim funeral was a subdued affair. After a short service at the funeral home, the congregation headed to the cemetery. It had drizzled all morning and the graveside, where they were gathered, was bitterly cold. Despite the weather there were about thirty five people present. Jeremy tipped his hat at Count Santinelli and Rachel noticed that the Count was escorted by a beautiful blonde lady in her early 30s. Rachel knew that she had seen her somewhere before but couldn't quite place her. Then it struck her that this was Madame Chartreuse, the same lady who had been interviewed by all the newspapers as the Countess' closest friend. A very good looking dark haired young man joined them just in time for the graveside service. He had not been present at the funeral home. Rachel realised that he had to be Count Santinelli's brother, Pietro – there was no mistaking the family resemblance.

Rachel and Jeremy stood slightly away from the main mourners or *avelim,* which as per Jewish tradition comprised of immediate family members. Although Aaron was neither family nor Jewish, he was standing beside Jonathan and Prudence Rosenheim, as the Rabbi read from the book of psalms.

The Rabbi then asked them all to observe a moment of silence. They stood in silence until he gave the signal to begin lowering the casket. As the casket was lowered in to its final resting place, he started chanting verses in Hebrew.

Rachel whispered to Jeremy that the casket was special. It was *kosher,* which meant that it was made entirely without the use of nails.

Jeremy nodded and whispered back, 'I see. By the way, do you know what he is chanting now?'

Rachel replied, 'Yes. It's called the *El Malei Rachamim.* Aaron told me that it is a rather beautiful prayer, which declares that the deceased is now 'sheltered beneath the wings of God's presence'.

After the chant came to an end, each member of the congregation took turns to put a handful of earth on to the casket in the ground as a final gesture of respect and closure.

The mourners then proceeded to the Shiva, which was to be held at the apartment on Rue Saint Dominique.

II

The apartment looked very different from her last visit. Rachel noticed that the numerous gilded mirrors, which had given that illusion of space and light, in the foyer and the sitting room, had been covered in black cloth. The rooms looked very different, smaller somehow. The gloom of the day made sure that even the light coming in through the French windows was grey and subdued. The whole effect seemed eerie and dark.

The sitting room was filled with subdued conversation as people milled about after paying their condolences to the grieving parents. When Rachel had finished paying her condolences to the Rosenheims, she noticed that Jeremy and Aaron were conversing at the far end of the room with Madame Chartreuse and the Count. Rachel did not know any of the other people who stood by in small groups speaking in hushed voices. She looked about her and on the mantelpiece, just to her left, she saw that a portrait of Isabelle had been placed alongside the large black and white family photograph, which Rachel had admired on her earlier visit. Isabelle's portrait was surrounded with candles. Curiosity got the better of her of and as she walked towards it, Rachel had a strange sensation that Isabelle's face seemed to come alive as the light from the flickering candles, animated her smile. She stopped a foot away from the picture and stood quietly, observing.

'Beautiful, wasn't she?' A man's deep voice said softly from behind. She hadn't heard anyone walk up to her. As Rachel turned slightly, she saw that it was the young man from the graveside, presumably, Pietro Santinelli. He was standing about a foot behind her, slightly to the right. Up close he was even more devastatingly handsome in a dangerous, masculine way. Even under his immaculate black suit, she could see that he was powerfully built. He towered over her.

Rachel looked at him sideways and replied softly, 'Yes, she was.' Then after a pause, she realised that he was still there. Without turning, she bent her head towards him and said casually, 'We haven't been introduced. I'm Rachel Markham.'

'Yes, I know who you are and I know why you are here,' he drawled, without ceremony. She realised that he had closed the distance between them and was now standing, just behind her right shoulder.

'You seem to know a lot,' she said evenly with a slight smile, not taking her eyes off the portrait.

'It's no secret that my brother hired you,' he said. Then coming closer, much closer, he bent his head slightly and put his lips near her ear and whispered softly in a deep voice, 'So, why haven't you harangued me yet?'

As his nose almost touched the nape of her neck and hair, his powerful body just an inch away, Rachel could smell his masculine scent and she felt an uncontrollable frisson of desire shoot through her. She felt momentarily disoriented, shocked at her own response towards this complete stranger. She turned around to look into his deep brown eyes and said softly, 'Now, why would I want to do that, Monsieur?'

She felt his penetrating gaze focus on her lips and then move up her face and lock onto her eyes, 'For pleasure, if nothing else,' he said in a thick voice. Despite her no nonsense view of the opposite sex, she felt her knees go weak. She couldn't help but stare back at him. The alarm must have shown in her eyes, because just then he moved away slightly, his eyes crinkling into a warm seductive smile. Then he turned around and simply walked away. Before she knew it, he was gone from the room.

She had heard of men like him, and she had read about men like him, men who had an animal magnetism and could make a woman melt, turn her into putty in their hands, in no time. But she realised that it was the first time in her life that she had encountered such a being, a real life Don Juan. And the very thought of their encounter brought a mysterious, unbidden smile to her face. She composed herself and then berated herself for behaving like a fool before making her way towards Jeremy, towards the familiar comfort of her husband's company.

She noticed that Jeremy was still standing with Madame Chartreuse at the far end of the room. Both were deep in conversation. The woman had her hand on his arm. Rachel noticed that Count Santinelli was nowhere to be seen. Something about Madame Chartreuse's body language and expressions gave Rachel the distinct impression that the French woman was using the full force of her charms on Jeremy. As she approached, Jeremy detached himself from the lady and smiled at Rachel as she joined them. Then putting his hand on the small of her back, in a proprietorial gesture, he introduced her to the woman. 'Rachel, you must meet this charming lady who has been keeping me company. Madame Chartreuse, may I introduce you to my wife.'

The charming lady gave her a quick head to toe appraisal and coming to the conclusion that Rachel was no significant threat to her own considerable allure, she said, 'Enchanté.' But before Rachel could respond, she moved away murmuring glibly in heavily accented English, 'Please do excuse me but I must meet some old friends.' She then floated away to another group of people in the room.

As Jeremy's eyes followed her, Rachel grinned and said, 'Sorry, darling. I didn't mean to scare off your new girlfriend.'

'Ah! The travails of being married! And just when things were getting somewhere with that heavenly creature.' Jeremy responded tongue-in-cheek before saying, 'Ouch!!' Rachel's pointy shoe had connected swiftly and playfully with his shin.

She remembered her own encounter with Pietro and the phrase, 'people who live in glass houses..', sprang to her mind, as they made their way towards the dining area.

Finger food had been placed on tables. Most of the arrangements were seen to by Aaron's personal assistant, a thin young man with spectacles, who was introduced to them earlier as Pierre Lambert. He seemed anxious and nervous at the same time as he handed everyone plates and serviettes. Rachel noticed that he kept looking towards Aaron for a sign of acknowledgement that he was doing a good job, while Aaron took no notice of him as he mingled with the guests. Suddenly she saw that Pierre stood frozen with a look of horror upon his face. She followed his gaze to the mantelpiece. It seemed to her that he was looking at the picture of Isabelle kept with candles lit around it. Something about it must have given him the shivers. In a minute, Pierre was almost back to normal and Rachel thought to herself that death had a strange and unnerving effect on certain people and thought nothing more of it.

She proceeded to give Jeremy an account of her brief encounter with the younger Santinelli sibling, naturally leaving out the embarrassing bit about how his charm had done a number on her. 'Oh, well, a girl has to have some secrets' she thought, smiling to herself, as they helped themselves to hors d'oeuvres.

Chapter Ten

The guests had departed and silence fell upon those who remained as if an invisible shroud was cast upon them. The candles were still flickering on the mantelpiece and throwing deep shadows around the room. Apart from the Rosenheims, Jeremy, Rachel and Aaron were the only ones left.

Aaron broke the silence. 'It's been quite a day.'

Jonathan Rosenheim gave him a bewildered look and then as if he was forcibly brought back from a distant horizon, he nodded but said nothing.

Jeremy spoke gently, 'I think we should all call it a day and leave you both to get some rest.'

Prudence shook her head and spoke, 'I don't think I can rest, not until I know why this happened. Such madness, such hatred towards my child. All for what? What did anyone achieve by her death? I just can't...'

Rachel who was seated next to her took her hand gently, 'You've been terribly brave Prudence but you must take courage for a little while longer. We know there is so much confusion, like a fog one can't see through at the moment but surely as the day comes, light will dawn and we will find out the "whys" and "hows" behind what happened.'

'How can you be so sure? What if we never find out?' Prudence asked.

Jeremy spoke, 'Oh we'll find out for sure, of that I have no doubt whatsoever. It is not the work of a mad man but of a very careful intelligence at work. Someone who has planned this carefully and executed both crimes flawlessly but in my experience, I believe that there is no such thing as a perfect crime. If one is dogged enough, sooner or later the truth comes out and we will catch him.'

'But how can you be certain that the killer was not a mad man, some random revolutionary from the streets of Montmartre?'

Jeremy responded, 'I know this because of my experience with psychological profiling. He is someone who probably wishes us to think that the crimes were committed by a mad man. But I am certain that the killer was known to both the victims and perhaps to you as well.

The meticulous care he took in not leaving any traces of himself, around both the crime scenes and making good his escape in a bustling neighbourhood without being noticed, goes to prove it. Furthermore, he got at both his victims not in some lonely street corner but in a place they both presumably felt safe, and where he could have been interrupted at any time leads me to believe that not only had he planned his moves well ahead in time but was probably not acting alone.'

Rachel spoke up, 'Why, Jeremy, I know that you and the Sûreté seem to think that both crimes were premeditated and not crimes of passion as they first believed but do you also think there was more than one person behind the crimes?'

Jeremy nodded, 'The deeper we delve into how the crimes were committed there seems to be a distinct possibility that the killer may have had an accomplice.'

Jonathan Rosenheim spoke in a weary voice, 'One can understand the motive behind killing the Countess. She held the keys to a great fortune but I simply cannot understand what anyone would gain by killing my daughter. Or do you have any theories for that too?'

Jeremy answered, 'I'm afraid the motives for both the crimes seem rather obscure at the moment but once we find the motives, we will get closer to finding the killers.'

Rachel nodded and asked Prudence, 'Would you know if Isabelle had any enemies in Paris? Anyone who could've wished her harm?'

'I should say not. We haven't been in France long enough!'

'Right. When did you last see her?' Rachel queried.

'She came by the night before she was ...' Prudence paused. 'We always dine together as a family on Fridays.'

'Did she seem normal to you that evening?' Jeremy asked.

'Normal? Yes, I suppose so. She was very quiet but then she was always soft spoken. She had never been a boisterous person to begin with, even before everything my children had to encounter and experience at the concentration camp, although that may have contributed to her reticence as an adult to a large extent.'

Rachel spoke, 'Did she have a special someone in her life, like a boyfriend or a close girlfriend?'

'If she did, she did not tell me. Daughters don't always tell their mothers everything, you know, and my Isabelle was a secretive girl to begin with. Not that she had anything to hide but some children are born that way. My son, Joel used to be the exact opposite. He would tell me everything,' Prudence replied with a faint smile.

Jonathan Rosenheim spoke, 'My dear, I think they will get further if we give them a list of people we know that she interacted with on a regular basis.' Then turning to Jeremy, he said, 'As far as I know, she knew Aaron of course and the people at the art gallery, some fellow artists, Aaron can give you their names. And the Santinellis and some of their friends – that Madame Chartreuse, for instance but we don't know if they were very close.'

Jeremy spoke, 'I read in the case files at the Sûreté that she was out walking with Pietro Santinelli the night his sister-in-law, the Countess was killed.'

Prudence responded, 'Yes, my daughter was fond of long walks. She said they inspired her art. In Paris, it is common to take walks with social acquaintances. That does not necessarily connote a closer friendship.'

Rachel said, 'No, I don't suppose it does but I think Jeremy meant to ask if she did things like that on a regular basis. Taking walks, going for art gatherings, parties, regular things like that? Was she outgoing?'

'Well yes and no. She did attend a few art gatherings mainly the ones Aaron threw. But I don't think she made friends easily. She was the type of person who kept to herself mostly, even in a room full of people. She was not very expressive but I felt that was the reason she took up painting and why she was so good at it. I suppose all those suppressed emotions had to come out somewhere. I believe that she allowed her work to speak for her. Have you seen any of her canvasses?'

'Not yet, but I would love to,' Rachel answered.

'Come with me.'

II

An hour later they had left the Rosenheim's apartment and as they made their way down to the foyer, Rachel and Jeremy realised to their chagrin that it was raining cats and dogs. The concierge was nowhere to be seen. Along with the missing concierge, went their hopes of sourcing an umbrella or getting a taxi. As they stood in the foyer wondering what to do next, moments later Aaron joined them and very kindly offered to give them a lift in his chauffeur driven car to the closest metro station.

'So, what did you think?' Aaron asked Rachel, as they sat together in the back seat. Jeremy had run out and opened the car door for her and then climbed into the passenger seat in front.

'About what?' Rachel asked turning away from the door to face Aaron.

'Isabelle's art, of course.'

'I thought it was quite good really. I don't claim to be an art expert but that painting with the two ladies taking an afternoon siesta by the river was quite picturesque. All that dappled sunlight playing through the trees - appealed to my romantic side immensely.'

'Yes that is rather good. One of her finest. Do you know who modelled for that?'

'I haven't the faintest. The faces were half covered with arms or hats. Besides, in their state of undress one can hardly expect the viewer to bother noticing their faces when everything else is put so delectably on display,' Rachel answered cheekily. 'Why do you ask?'

Aaron smiled mysteriously but said nothing. Rachel rolled her eyes and said, 'Oh, come on, Aaron. Now that you've got my curiosity piqued, you may as well tell me.'

Aaron gave a wink in Rachel's direction and prodded Jeremy in the front seat, 'Perhaps, you recognised one of them, Monsieur Richards?'

'Eh, what?' Jeremy turned around, confused.

Rachel explained, 'Aaron seems to think you may have recognised one of the models in the painting...'

'Which painting?'

Rachel responded, 'The one with the two women taking their forty winks by the river.'

Aaron added with a cheeky grin, 'Surely, you remember. Most men would.'

'Haven't the foggiest notion what you two are on about,' was Jeremy's response as the car swerved on the rain slicked road, the chauffeur honked and continued making his way through Parisian traffic.

Rachel suddenly realised why Aaron was enjoying himself so much at her expense. 'Why, you old devil!' She said with a grin, narrowing her eyes at Aaron. 'One of them is Madame Chartreuse, isn't it?'

'Ma cherie, I salute your womanly instincts. Yes, Viola was the blonde lady with her arm over her forehead.'

'Hmm, I see and that voluptuous red head besides her with her hand on Viola's er..bosom?'

'Why that was Sarah, Countess Santinelli of course.'

'Oh really ? How interesting.'

'Strange you should say that.'

'Why?'

'When that painting was exhibited it created quite a furore. Critics said that the artist had intentionally given the scene a diabolical touch of sexuality. That there was more to its depiction than just an innocent siesta. As if the artist had wanted to deliberately convey that the two women were lovers.'

'And were they?' Rachel asked with one raised eyebrow.

'My dear, you mustn't draw me into a potentially dangerous social quagmire,' he replied with a grin. 'Perhaps you ought to ask Viola that question.'

Rachel smiled and retorted, 'Perhaps I shall. Tell me more about her, Viola, I mean. All I know about her so far, is that she is a wealthy widow.'

'Oh yes, ma cherie, one hears that she was devastated when her rich, old, pernickety husband died leaving her, his entire estate. They say that within a month of his passing, her hair turned quite gold with grief,' he informed her with a straight face.

'Aaron, you really are an old devil!' Rachel spluttered through her laughter.

'Less of the old, ma cherie, s'il vous plait,' he said with mock anguish as the car stopped in front of their desired disembarkation point - the metro station entrance.

Chapter Eleven

The next day Jeremy left early to update Inspector Didier Lachaille about his shadowing Suzette Bouvier.

'She has a child? Are you sure?' Didier asked, surprised.

'Yes, a boy, about five or six years old.'

'There is no mention of it in our files. Are you sure the child is hers? We do know she has a sister living in the suburbs. We French, are, how you say, affectionate people. Perhaps, you saw her greeting her sister's child.'

'No, Didier. Even affectionate French boys don't go running about calling their aunts "Maman" however close they may be.'

'There is that. And then you say there was a Gladstone bag she picked up the Pont Marie. It could be a bag of clothes or personal items. Something innocent like that.'

'No, she picked up the bag at Gare de l'Est. And I should think that if her son has been living at her sister's house for quite some time, she would already have a few personal items stored there. No, I think there was something else in that bag and it was not clothes. She treated it with far too much care for that.'

'That does sound interesting. You think perhaps it could be a payout of some kind,' Didier said, his eyes twinkling.

Jeremy smiled back. He was once again impressed with the Inspector's quick uptake and razor sharp intelligence. Jeremy said, 'Look, I may be wrong but if it is a payout of some sort, that Gladstone would probably hold enough to set her son and her up for life.'

'I can't possibly arrest her again based on this,' Didier sighed.

'Well, no but if I were you, I'd get a search warrant and find out what it contains. Worse comes to worst, we'll come away shamefaced but enlightened. And on an optimistic note, if we do find that it is a payout of some sort, you may be able to unravel this case in record time.'

Didier looked at him steadily and then rang a bell on his desk. Moments later a smartly uniformed gendarme came in. The inspector scribbled something on a chit of paper and handed it over to the young man with a sharp instruction. 'Tout de suite!'

As the gendarme left, Jeremy asked with a raised eyebrow, 'Don't tell me that you've already requested a search warrant?'

'Non, Monsieur Richards. I have asked him to go through birth records in Paris from 1941 to 1944 and get me a particular record that carries the name of the mother as Suzette Bouvier.'

'Right. Oh, and I wanted to ask you if the toxicology report came in?'

'As a matter of fact it did,' Didier said, as he pushed a file across the desk towards Jeremy. 'It seems that they found traces of veronal. Just as we had in the first murder.'

'That is interesting.'

'Yes, it blows away our theory that these were crimes of passion. This murder too was well thought out. In the Countess' case, we weren't as sure as we were informed by two of her close associates, including her husband that she was in the habit of taking veronal. But we know for sure that is not the case with Isabelle Rosenheim. Her parents were quite certain that she would never touch veronal. It was a sensitive topic.'

'Yes, I know. It has been for thousands of Jews, ever since Victor Klemperer labelled veronal as "Jewish drops". But my question is, why drug the victim, if you were about to slit her throat?'

Didier shrugged his shoulders, 'Less resistance? Also an unconscious victim cannot fight back.'

'Yes but why slit the throat? Why not just stab or strangle instead? Or administer a lethal dose and let the Veronal do its job in its entirety?'

'Ah, that I do not know as yet, Monsieur.'

'Or, and this is just a thought, perhaps this style of killing, twice in a row, is an indication that the killer wants to leave his signature. Back at Scotland Yard, I remember that we hunted down an assassin whose signature killing style was removing the victim's little finger. He had quite a collection of gruesome souvenirs in his refrigeration unit by the time we caught up with him. '

'Yes, Monsieur, as you say that is also a possibility. I'll have them check all homicide records in Paris for the past three years to see if we can up with a match for this particular "signature".'

II

Meanwhile at the hotel, just as Rachel had finished breakfast, she was informed that she had a telephone call. It was Aaron Berger.

He sounded cheery. 'What are you doing this evening, ma cherie?'

'Nothing very exciting. Just planning a quiet evening with my husband, supper at our hotel and an early night.'

'No. You both are going to join me at my gallery for a magnificent viewing of some old masters I've managed to recently source. A Seurat, a Courbet. Also a magnificent little piece painted over a photograph of a lithograph by none other than Henri Toulouse-Lautrec.'

'That does sound interesting but I must confess that I'm not much of an art enthusiast. I mean I do like art but I don't really know what makes the old masters so significant. And for the life of me, I can't tell the difference between a Rembrandt and a street artist's version of a Rembrandt.'

'Mon Dieu! We must take measures to correct this terrible fallacy in your otherwise almost perfect persona. I cannot possibly let you go through the remainder of your life in such ignorance. We must correct it immediately! Meet me at the Louvre, in front of the Mona Lisa in forty minutes.' He hung up before Rachel could make any excuse.

III

An hour later, Rachel was being jostled by a crowd of sightseers in the hallowed hall of the Louvre that showcased Da Vinci's masterpiece. There was a gentle tap on her shoulder and as she whirled around, Aaron stood there, impeccably dressed with an enigmatic smile on his lips. 'Come, let me show you something special.'

They walked in silence through galleries and finally came to stop in front of a small oil on an oak panel. It wasn't very large, a rectangle of just a foot and a half by a foot. To Rachel's mind it seemed dwarfed by the huge paintings they had just passed.

Aaron spoke with deep reverence, 'This is a Rembrandt. It was painted in 1640 and acquired by the Louvre, a century later in 1793. The painting is called 'Holy Family' but what makes it truly holy is the way he has played with the light. Look and observe. I want you to look at it through childlike eyes as if you were seeing it through a baby's new eyes and absorb the light.'

Rachel did. The painting depicted a young mother breastfeeding her child bathed in a stream of sunlight that came in through an open window. There were two other people in the room, one looking upon the child, affectionately adjusting the shawl around the baby and a man with his back to them, casually working on something. Rachel observed that while the rest of the room was dingy by any standards, the light that pooled around the mother and child, elevated them to a state of grace. And it struck her that the wonder of it was that it could have just as easily been portrayed as a direct beam of blessing from a smiling God but instead the light was portrayed so naturally and with such ease, it reflected playfully around them and glistened upon the old wooden floor boards, bringing the image vibrantly to life. As she stared, the din of the sightseers around her started fading away and she felt herself being transported into that room, as though some of that light reflected on her as well. She was a disembodied entity standing in that very room, no longer merely an art observer, standing centuries away viewing an artwork in a museum but as though she had entered this space of light and become a part of it. She found herself being drawn in to it, as if by invitation from a higher power. She felt a tremendous sense of peace and calm descend upon her. How long she stood in that room watching the mother and child, she did not know.

She felt a gentle tap on her shoulder and within a fraction of a second, she was once more back in the Louvre, just another art observer.

She slowly turned to look at Aaron, her eyes shining.

He looked at her knowingly and nodded. 'Yes. I think you are beginning to understand. You see, Rachel, it is like this with cherished works of the masters. They were not ordinary people. They elevated art to a level where the soul could perceive greatness and allow the mind to roam the empyrean – a place a rare few have had the privilege to visit in the history of mankind.'

'I don't know what to say.'

He continued, 'This is why I work in the art world and help people acquire old Masters. I could not dream of doing anything better. You see, it is my life's work to show collectors that possessing a Master goes beyond mere acquisition of a material thing. It is man's ultimate hope of entering a sacred world, where one can let one's imagination freely roam in a realm seen only through a Master's eye, by the touch of his hand and the magic of his soul. All lying bare in the art work, waiting to be discovered by those who have eyes to see, and a heart to perceive.'

Rachel nodded as they walked and asked, 'But how does one tell a Master's work from a forged copy? Surely there are enough instances of counterfeit artwork being of such fine quality that it is difficult for even art experts to tell the difference? I've heard it said that even the pigments used are as dated as the original and that even museum curators get fooled into purchasing forgeries. There was that much publicised incident at the Prado in Madrid just before the war broke.'

'Yes, there are such incidents but the true art connoisseur will know when he is in the presence of an original Master. The work itself has a certain soul. And if one looks deeply, the true art lover will know instinctively the difference between an original and a seemingly flawless copy. You must understand that when you are finally in the presence of a thing of immense beauty and power from an unfathomable realm, a door opens.'

'At the risk of sounding rather dim-witted, I'm afraid you've lost me there.'

'How can I put it? It is almost as though the door, which was previously closed now slowly creeks open, barely a crack but enough to give one, a glimpse of another world – another level of a higher soul. That, my dear, is the magic that a Rembrandt, a Vermeer, a Gauguin, a Van Gogh and luckily for us, the list is long – bring to the world.'

'Aaron, hearing you speak like that makes me want to simply dash out and burgle a bank, to buy an original master from you. You have such a gift. Your art dealership must be doing rather well.'

'I can't complain. And I can't possibly imagine making a living doing anything else. Though I must admit, between you and me, the past year has been rather good. Surpassed my own expectations, even. '

'Really?'

'Yes and surprisingly so. One did expect an improvement once the war ended but originals seem to be coming on to the market with frightening speed.'

'I see. Tell me Aaron, where do you source your paintings from?'

'Now that will be akin to opening my Pandora's box and letting out all my well guarded trade secrets!'

'Oh, please don't get me wrong, I don't mean to pry but I've always wondered where the really influential art dealers, people like yourself, for instance, source valuable old paintings from. Is it from estate auctions, or distress sales from suddenly impoverished nobility or do you rely on individuals and other lesser art dealers to acquire artwork?'

'You aren't planning to open an art gallery in London anytime soon, are you?'

Rachel laughed, 'Not a chance. I don't have the money and even if I managed to sweet talk someone into investing, I would probably end up buying every fake that comes on the market.'

Aaron laughed. 'Well, seeing as you aren't a potentially competitive threat, I will tell you that you are on the right track. It is a combination of all the sources you mentioned. You see, sometimes I am approached by old families staggering under the burden of heavy death duties and I help them, very discreetly, to dispose some old family treasures. And I also get offers to buy from middlemen whose job is to scout around the countryside and pick up artwork from old estates under sale. The war years were rather slack but now there seems to be a rush to get rid of old things. People who are moving on to newer homes or redoing their original ones tend to throw out the things that have been in their attic for generations without giving it so much as a second glance. And in this mad rush to modernise everything post war, I seem to have benefitted enormously.'

'I'll say! That does sound interesting. Well, good for you, Aaron.'

Chapter Twelve

Jeremy returned to the hotel just as Rachel was asking for their room key. They met in the foyer and he gave her a peck on her cheek and said, 'You've been out.'

'Yes, I've just been on a most informative Rembrandt tour around the Louvre with Aaron Berger.'

'I say! That old boy seems to be dotty over you. I had better watch my step,' Jeremy said with a grin.

'Don't be mean, Jeremy. He is a nice man,' Rachel replied with a smile, as they walked arm in arm towards the stairs.

'Did the nice man tell you about the Rembrandt of dubious fame that he almost sold to the Countess before her death?'

'No, the nice man also happens to be a shrewd one. He seems to be warming towards me, although he's still a bit dodgy about where he gets his paintings from but don't you worry, I'll worm it out of him sooner or later.'

'Atta girl!'

'And I want to play my cards just right so I don't scare him away before I find out exactly who supplies him with the masters,' Rachel said, as they reached the door to their room.

'And what cards would those be, my beautiful? Or need I ask,' Jeremy said with a sardonic smile as he turned the key and held the door open for her.

Rachel giggled as she sashayed into the room and flung her handbag on the settee. 'Jeremy Richards! Behave yourself. At the moment I'm playing the I-know-nothing-about-art card and he's taken the bait - hook, line and sinker. He's taken it upon himself to be my art avuncular.'

'I think he'll be mighty chuffed when he finds out you went to finishing school at Switzerland and art appreciation is about the only useful thing they teach at those places. Does he know that you spent a year in Florence and know the Uffizi like the back of your hand?'

'No, he doesn't and I'd like to keep it that way, thank you very much. Don't you go about dropping hints about my alleged knowledge about art. I'm a babe in the woods as far as he's concerned.'

'I wouldn't dream of interfering with your nefarious schemes, my darling. As long as you don't waste too much time on art lessons. We do have a case to solve here, you know.'

'Oh! But my morning wasn't a total waste of time, Jeremy. There is something that may be of interest to you – he claims that over the past year, original Masters seem to be popping out of the woodwork all of a sudden at estate sales in the countryside and so on and so forth.'

'Hmm. That could be a convenient explanation to cover his involvement in a counterfeiting ring, you know. Be careful, my love.'

'I will but he insists he sells only originals and that he can spot a fake, a mile away,' she said, taking off her pumps and making herself comfortable on an armchair.

'Darling, in all my years at the Yard, I never met an art counterfeiter but I'm quite sure that if I had, he would have used the very same words. Confidence tricksters the world over are known to possess a great deal of charm and come across as thoroughly reliable people. And they can generally charm an Eskimo into buying a refrigeration unit. It's a gift. I hate to disillusion you but your man seems to fit the bill.'

'I must admit I shall be disappointed if he turns out to be one but that isn't what bothers me. After all, if he is at the center of a forgery ring, we may find a connection to solving the murders. I'm just wondering how we can get hold of one of his "masters" so that a real art expert can verify its authenticity without arousing Aaron's suspicions.'

Just then telephone rang and Jeremy walked over to pick it up. 'Yes?' And then his face broke into a smile, as an exchange of greetings took place. He covered the mouthpiece and said to Rachel, 'Darling, it's your mother.'

Rachel glanced at him and then jumped up. 'My mother! That's it! She could do it. I could cry with pride at my flashes of brilliance,' Rachel said, as she took the phone from a very puzzled Jeremy.

Rachel spoke, barely able to control her excitement, 'Mummy darling, I am so glad you called. I have a very interesting job for you. How soon can you get to Paris?'

II

Meanwhile at La Crim, a gendarme knocked and entered Inspector Didier Lachaille's room and handed him a sheet of paper. It was a copy of a birth certificate. It stated plainly that Suzette Bouvier had given birth to a baby boy on February 22nd, 1942. The father was listed as unknown.

February 1942 rang a bell in Didier's mind and then he remembered why. It had been recorded as being the single coldest month in the history of France since 1895. An unusual cold front had swept the nation. Temperatures had been freezing, consistently at -12 C and below. Severe sleet and snow had brought life in Paris to a standstill. He remembered that there had been reports of several people being found frozen to death and ironically this poor fatherless child had chosen that very month to enter the world. He felt a tinge of sympathy for both mother and child. Such was life. He sighed and then putting aside his personal thoughts, Didier sprang into action.

Two and a half hours later, he was on his way to Bobigny with a party of two gendarmes and a valid search warrant.

By five o'clock in the evening, he was knocking on the door of the house, the address of which was listed in their files as belonging to Anna Marie Bouvier, Suzette Bouvier's sister. A tired looking woman in her thirties answered the door. She was wearing a dirty apron and her hands were covered in flour. She had evidently been busy in the kitchen. She looked up suspiciously at them. Didier introduced himself matter-of-factly and handed her the search warrant. She dusted her hands on her already smudged apron and read the warrant. She then moved aside without a word and let them in.

Didier gave instructions in his usual staccato fashion that they were to look for a dark brown leather Gladstone bag. The gendarmes went to work. Anna Marie returned to her kitchen with a weary step. Didier looked around the dingy rooms and opened several closets on the ground floor but found no sign of the Gladstone. The gendarmes also came back downstairs, within fifteen minutes to report that they were unable to locate it or anything of a similar description. Didier sighed. He asked them to wait outside and followed the smell of a pie baking in the oven. She was sitting quietly at the worn old kitchen table. Didier noticed that she had washed her hands and tidied her appearance. It seemed to him that she had been waiting for him.

He asked her in French whether she minded if he sat down. She shook her head and motioned him to take the chair in front of her. He complimented her on the aroma emanating from the oven and she gave him a wan smile. She told him that she baked pies for a living and that she supplied supper for the lodgers next door. But then, she added with a hint of a smile that an important man like him wouldn't have come all the way with a search warrant for that information. Didier was amused and he fancied he saw a twinkle in her eye. She almost looked pretty at that moment. But he shook his head and came straight to the point. He told her what he was looking for and asked her where Suzette and her boy were.

She sighed and told him that they were gone and that Suzette had left no forwarding address but she had promised to send her a post card soon. No, she did not know where Suzette had planned to go.

Anna Marie informed him that Suzette had had a visitor two days ago. She didn't know his name but gave Didier a description. Apparently he had seemed like a perfectly ordinary young man of average height, in his early twenties, a bit on the thinner side and of somewhat pale complexion. He hadn't looked very threatening to her but his visit had left Suzette shaken to a point where she had packed her bags and taken Étienne – her son, to the railway station within an hour of the man's departure.

Didier asked if she recalled seeing a brown Gladstone bag. She nodded and said that just before she left, Suzette had opened it and handed her a thousand francs from the bag. Didier cursed under his breath. He had come too late. He thanked her and gave her his card. He requested her to give him a call as soon as she got wind of her sister's current whereabouts and he promised her that he would protect both Suzette and the little boy, if she helped him.

She nodded and he finally got up to take his leave and then as an afterthought he asked her if he could have a slice of one of her pies and told her politely that he would be happy to pay. She got up and carefully made a parcel of food for him and handed it to him with compliments of the house. After all she could afford to, she said. Thanks to her sister, she was a thousand francs richer. And there was that twinkle in her eye again.

Chapter Thirteen

The invitation said seven o'clock but by the time Jeremy and Rachel reached the Berger Art Galerie, it was seven thirty and they found quite a crowd around the entrance. Rachel noticed that once they checked in their coats, the women were extremely well turned out and some chic young French women were flaunting the season's latest fashions. She was glad that she had overcome her fear of being overdressed and had decided to wear her classic yet flamboyant ankle length Molyneux burgundy silk. Her hair was swept into a top knot and she was aware of several eyes following her as she and Jeremy made their way towards Aaron.

He broke away from the group of people he was standing with and greeted them. 'My dear, you look absolutely sensational. People will want introductions and I hope your husband will not mind,' he said to Rachel with unconcealed admiration in his eyes. Then he turned to Jeremy, smiled and held out his hand.

Jeremy shook his hand and responded, 'Not in the least, old chap. Introduce away. You seem to have quite a party going on here.'

'Ah, yes. It is always like this when there are Masters on display. But first you must have a glass of champagne,' he said, stopping a passing waiter and handing them champagne flutes. 'I am pleased to say that some of the richest people in Europe have decided to grace my humble Galerie tonight. Come let me introduce you to one,' he said, as he led the way towards a group of people admiring a Seurat.

He singled out a tall blond man in his forties with Nordic features and ice blue eyes and addressed him. 'Freidrich, I'd like to introduce you to friends of mine from across the Channel. This beautiful young lady is Rachel and this is her husband, Jeremy Richards.'

The man in question responded with a smile that did not quite reach his cold eyes. He said in a clipped voice with a slight German accent, 'I am always happy to meet your friends, Aaron.'

Then turning towards Rachel, Aaron said, 'And it is my pleasure to introduce you to Freidrich von Schmidt, one of my oldest patrons and a great art collector. His magnificent homes in Switzerland and Austria are rumoured to house the largest private collection of Renaissance Masters and Impressionists outside of a museum.'

Rachel spoke, 'How fascinating.'

Jeremy shook his hand, 'Pleased to meet you. Tell me, aside from collecting art what is it you do, Mr. von Schmidt? I seem to recollect having heard of you, yet I am quite sure it was not in relation with your art collection, which sounds quite formidable, by the way.'

'Ah, I have several business interests, Mr. Richards. Art is merely a passionate hobby of mine. And what is it that you do?'

Jeremy responded self-effacingly, 'I am just a retired old fogey, I'm afraid. I spend most of my days doing a lot of nothing.'

Rachel spoke, 'You mustn't believe him Mr. von Schmidt. My husband used to be with the Scotland Yard and now he is a private investigator.'

'I see. And you are here in Paris for business or pleasure?'

'A bit of both,' Jeremy said. 'I seem to be on a busman's holiday. Apart from taking in the sights and sounds of Paris, my wife and I are both involved in investigating Countess Santinelli's murder.'

'Ah, yes. Sarah – I knew her well. Charming woman. Such a pity she was killed. Paris is not the same without her. I wish you both luck in your endeavour but now I must excuse myself. I have an early morning train to catch.'

Aaron asked, 'Are you heading back to Switzerland?'

Schmidt replied, 'No, I have to attend to some business in Austria. I shall return next week. Aaron, I think you are wanted over there.' He pointed towards Pierre Lambert. Aaron excused himself and joined Pierre, who was beckoning him to join another group of people.

As von Schmidt made a motion to depart, Rachel suddenly asked, 'So are you planning to invest in the Seurat?'

'No Madame, these Masters are from my collection and Aaron here is helping me to offload some of my paintings.'

'If it's not too forward of me, may I ask why are you selling?'

'Not at all. I have far too many paintings and these have been lying in my vault for years. I had bought these purely from a point of investment. It is simply a good time to sell. Now if you'll excuse me, I must take my leave. It was good to meet you both,' he said and walked away without ceremony.

Rachel gave Jeremy a meaningful glance. 'Well, that certainly answers one of our questions.'

'Yes, it does. You know, my love, I can't help thinking that I've heard his name somewhere but where and in what connection... perhaps I'm going senile.'

'Well, darling, if it makes you feel any better, I can't remember what I had for breakfast.'

'That's reassuring; the knowledge that we are both going senile together.'

Rachel laughed, 'I'm sure it will come to you but to be on the safe side, why don't you ask your chums at the Sûreté to give you a head's up? He seems to be quite a well known figure in Paris.'

'What a good idea. I say, let's get away from here. I'm feeling a bit peckish. We can go across the street and grab a spot to eat and I can make that telephone call.'

'Jeremy, that would be rude. We haven't been here long enough. Let's at least go and look at a few sculptures and paintings before we bolt.'

They were introduced to several people whom they exchanged pleasantries with. Madame Chartreuse was conspicuous in her absence. Rachel observed that Pietro Santinelli was present and busy charming the same fashionable young French women she had noticed earlier. He caught her eye and gave her a smile and a wave from across the room. Rachel nodded back in acknowledgment and looked away.

Count Santinelli came up and met them. He looked quite pleased with himself and informed them that he had just bought the oriental sculpture on display in one of the private viewing rooms upstairs. They followed him upstairs as he led the way to show them his new art acquisition. It was a life sized sculpture of a stern old Japanese warrior holding a Samurai sword. Rachel and Jeremy made appreciative noises. As the Count walked away to greet another couple in the room, Jeremy, whispered in her ear, 'Ugly looking bloke, isn't he?'

She giggled and whispered back, 'And here I was hoping you'd get me something like this for Christmas.'

By the time they finally decided to leave, they looked around for Aaron but couldn't find him. Rachel spotted Pierre Lambert and told Jeremy, 'I won't be a minute. You go and get our coats and I'll leave a thank you note for our host.'

Pierre Lambert seemed nervous as Rachel gave him a message for Aaron. Then looking about him furtively, he took her to one side and said in a hushed voice, 'I saw you talking to that man earlier. There is something going on. I can't speak now. It's too dangerous but I need to talk to you.' Then he surreptitiously placed a piece of paper in her hand and whispered, 'Keep this. I'll explain later.'

Two minutes later, Rachel joined Jeremy and they made their way to the restaurant right across the street from the Berger Art Galerie.

Chapter Fourteen

The head waiter was very charming, 'May I suggest la soupe à l'oignon and the escargot, Madame. We received a fresh batch from Marseilles this very evening. Followed by our restaurant's famous Chateaubriand and a bottle of vintage Bordeaux from our excellent wine cellar. I am sure Monsieur will appreciate it. And for dessert I offer you our house specialty - Crème brulée à la Vanille'

Rachel smiled at him. 'Oh, yes that sounds quite perfect, merci.'

As the head waiter left their table, Jeremy got up to make the phone call. Rachel opened her clutch to read the piece of paper that Pierre Lambert had passed into her hand earlier. It seemed to be an address in Montmartre.

She puzzled over it then folded it and put it back. Jeremy returned.

Rachel looked up. 'That was quick.'

'I couldn't reach Didier or Henri. Apparently they've just been called away on another murder case. I'll try again in the morning.'

By the time they were on their escargot, they heard a great deal of commotion on the street outside.

Jeremy called a passing waiter to ask what was going on. He informed them casually that it was nothing. Just some trouble at the art gallery across the street. Apparently, someone had been killed there.

They both scraped back their chairs and jumped up. Rachel was horror struck, 'Oh my God! I hope it isn't Aaron!'

Jeremy left enough money on the table and told the astonished waiter to pack the rest of their meal and that they would collect it later.

As they pushed their way through the throng that had collected outside and re-entered the Galerie, Jeremy immediately spotted the lanky Henri Beauchamp. He introduced Rachel to him and asked, 'What's happened?'

'A Galerie employee – a man called Pierre Lambert was found dead in one of the upstairs rooms, with a sword like thing stuck through him. It seems the murder weapon was part of a sculpture.'

'Good Lord!' And then referring to the din coming from the next room Jeremy asked, 'What's with all the noise?'

Henri shrugged his shoulders and explained, 'Some girls found him. They had gone upstairs to powder their noses and stumbled upon the body. They haven't stopped screaming since. Hysterical women! Didier has been trying to calm them down ever since we got here, poor man.'

'Where's Aaron Berger?' Rachel asked.

'Who?'

Rachel replied unable to hide the impatience in her voice, 'Surely you must know - the man who owns the gallery.'

'Oh, yes. He seems to have gone missing. How do you both know him?'

Jeremy answered, 'It's a long story. Suffice to say he invited us for this event he was very much present up until an hour ago.'

'And that is the last time you saw him?'

'Yes.'

'And what about Pierre Lambert?'

'We saw him alive and well, just before we left to get a bite to eat shortly after eight. We went across the road to that restaurant,' Jeremy said, pointing to the establishment through the Gallery's plate glass windows.

'So that narrows down the window of the crime. I had better start rounding up people for enquiries.'

'I don't envy you. There must have been close to a hundred people in the Gallery at the time the crime was committed.'

'Yes and this is yet another bold crime. This time the murderer took an immense risk. I don't understand it.'

'Perhaps he was desperate to try and stop Pierre from revealing something.'

'Still. He could have waited till the guests had departed.'

'Or perhaps he chose his moment well and then melted into the crowd. He could be watching us smugly, even as we speak.'

The inspector said gloomily, 'This is going to look bad for us if we don't make an arrest tonight. I had better get moving.'

Jeremy spoke. 'Look Henri, I know you are dreadfully busy and all that but can you tell me if you've heard of a chap called Friedrich von Schmidt? He was here too this evening.'

Henri whistled under his breath. 'He is a big gun. Runs a cargo shipping line among other things. We've had our eye on him for a while. Didier suspects he's at the helm of an underground fascist organisation here in Paris but we haven't been able to find any proof of it yet. Why do you ask?'

'Ah, yes! The Northern Cargo Company. Now I remember where I had heard of him! It was at the Yard. He was also rumoured to have nobbled arms shipments to the Allied forces during the war. Faulty guns and bombs that wouldn't go off - that sort of thing but although his shipping service came under suspicion, we couldn't pin anything on him back then. Just as in this case - no proof.'

'What has he got to do, with what happened here?'

'Probably nothing but I suspect he could also be at the helm of a large scale art counterfeiting ring. Just a tip – get that Seurat displayed on that wall over there, checked for authenticity.'

Just then a gendarme came in through a door that connected to the inner offices and informed the inspector that the gallery owner – Monsieur Berger had been found unconscious behind the desk in the back office. And that he had telephoned for the ambulance.

Rachel spoke beseechingly, 'May I see him? Please?'

Henri looked uncertain and glanced at Jeremy. Jeremy understood the inspector's dilemma and answered for him, 'Darling, I think it best to let the medical staff handle the situation. And I'm sure the police don't want anyone going into the back office until the forensic team is done collecting evidence. If Aaron was attacked there, it is technically a part of the crime scene.'

As if on cue, Didier came out of the next room and announced in French that if anyone had seen anything of consequence pertaining to the murder they were requested to give their statements to the police now. Aside from that, those who had seen or heard nothing, excepting the gallery employees were to give their addresses and contact details to the gendarmes and that they would be contacted in the morning to give an account of their movements. Meanwhile the police would have to clear the gallery so that the forensic team could get to work.

II

Rachel and Jeremy gave their statements and then headed back to their hotel after picking up their parcel from the restaurant. They managed to bribe the parlourmaid into lending them some plates, wine glasses and cutlery. They made themselves comfortable in front of the fire in their room and ate their cold dinner.

Rachel spoke as Jeremy uncorked the Bordeaux and poured her a glass. 'Jeremy, I held back the piece of paper from the police. You know, the one that Pierre Lambert, God rest his soul, handed to me just before he was killed. Here it is. What do you make of it?'

'It's an address in Montmartre.'

'I can see that but what do you suppose he was trying to tell me?'

'I don't know - that depends on what he told you, prior to handing you that piece of paper.'

'Well, he mentioned something about a man he had seen us talking to and he said something about things not being right and that it was too dangerous to talk there. He gave me the paper and said he'd explain later. I didn't ask him which man since we met quite a few people. I was in a hurry, you see and you were waiting for me so I thought I'd ask him later. Silly me, I know, but how was I to know that he would go and get himself murdered, just moments later?'

'He could have been referring to von Schmidt or Count Santinelli or even Aaron Berger. Those were the only three men we spoke with for any length of time. The rest was just superfluous socialising.'

'Yes. But which one? On second thought I doubt if he would refer to Aaron as 'that man'. I think it's a toss-up between the Count and von Schmidt. My instincts tell me that he was referring to the latter.'

Jeremy said, 'I think we ought to go and see what's at this address before we jump to any conclusions.'

'Yes you are right, darling. We'll do that first thing in the morning.'

'I'm afraid we both may have to go and meet the inspector first thing in the morning but we could visit this address on our way back.'

'Alright. But in this entire episode, there is one thing that I find rather odd.'

'And what might that be, my love?'

'The fact that the poor man was killed by the sword held by that warrior – the one you admired so much. Who would have thought that the sword was real?'

Chapter Fifteen

Rachel and Jeremy were at La Crim the next morning as planned. Jeremy was about to knock on Didier Lachaille's door when the door was suddenly flung opened and a harried Gendarme came out and ran past them. They heard the sound of raised voices from within. Jeremy poked his head in and asked, 'Is this a bad time?'

'Oui! It is a most terrible time!' Didier said with a dramatic gesture. 'I am forced to work with fier imbeciles! Come in. Do you know what has happened?'

Jeremy shook his head, 'Afraid, not.'

'That idiot who just went out was supposed to be keeping a night watch at the Gallery. Now he comes and informs me that some burglars broke in, in the early morning hours and stole some paintings. From right under his nose. Imbecile! If we weren't so short handed, I would have sacked him,' he shouted.

Henri Beauchamp was in the room too and he silently motioned Rachel to take a seat.

Jeremy said, 'That is bad news but wait a minute, did he tell you which paintings were taken?'

'The ones on display last evening. And now I learn that they are very valuable. Merde! The fool must have gone to sleep. The back door of the Gallery was forced open. Luckily, only the three paintings were removed.'

Jeremy offered, 'Strange that the burglars only targeted the paintings on display.'

'But Monsieur, they were the most valuable ones in the gallery!'

'Or my other theory holds good that they were counterfeit and the people concerned had them removed before you could test them for authenticity. With the publicity the Gallery was bound to receive from the press owing to the murder, they probably thought it was a better idea to take the paintings out before someone decided to take a closer look at them!'

'Mon Dieu! I had not thought of that.'

Jeremy addressed Rachel, 'Darling, I think it's time you shared that note Pierre Lambert gave you with the Inspector.'

Didier asked, 'Comment? Which note?'

Rachel took it out of her purse and explained.

The inspector said, 'We'll look into it but later. For now, we need to question the owner of the gallery. I've just got word from the hospital that he has recovered.

II

Rachel was the first to enter the hospital room followed by Jeremy and the two inspectors.

She walked over to his bed side and took his hand, 'Aaron, you had me scared. I am so thankful that you are feeling better.'

Aaron Berger was looking rather sorry for himself but he managed a smile, 'It is always a pleasure to see you, ma cherie. More so, after this terrible night. It is very kind of you to visit.'

Rachel spoke, 'The Inspector very kindly allowed me to come and see you. He is here and he would like to ask you a few questions if you are up to it.'

Aaron nodded.

Didier pulled up a chair and came straight to the point. 'Monsieur Berger, the toxicology report is not in yet but the doctor suspects that you have recovered from a large dose of some sleeping drug. Do you know how it was administered to you?'

'I was drugged?'

'Apparently.'

'But I ate nothing last night.'

Rachel spoke, 'It could have been in your champagne glass. I do remember you had some champagne with us last night.'

'But I took it off a tray and you both had the same champagne.'

Rachel asked, 'Do you remember putting your glass down anywhere?'

'I probably did, several times through the evening but my memory is still a little hazy.'

The inspector spoke, 'You were found unconscious in your office. Do you remember why you went there?'

'Yes, I seem to remember Pierre informing me that I had an important telephone call from one of my suppliers regarding a high value shipment.'

'And was there someone with you?'

'No, I don't think so.'

'I will need the name of the supplier to verify the call.'

'Why do you need the name of the supplier? Why not just ask my assistant, Monsieur Lambert and he will corroborate my story. Besides, I am the victim here, why should I lie?'

The two inspectors exchanged glances and Didier spoke, 'I am afraid we cannot question Pierre Lambert. He was found dead last night at your gallery.'

'What? Why has nobody told me about this? Rachel, is this true?'

Rachel nodded, 'I'm afraid so, Aaron.'

'What is going on? Are you telling me that I was drugged and my assistant was murdered?'

The inspector responded, 'Yes, Monsieur. It would seem so. Now if you would care to give me the name of the supplier.'

'I am sorry. I cannot remember.'

'You cannot remember the name of this supplier whose call was so important that you dropped everything you were doing at your busy event, just to take his call?'

'No, I cannot.'

'Are you sure you even went in to take a telephone call?'

'Look here, Inspector, I refuse to be treated like a criminal and if you insist on doing so, I too insist on having my advocate present should you wish to interrogate me any further.'

'You are well within your rights to do so. Monsieur Aaron Berger, I hereby arrest you for the murder of your assistant, Pierre Lambert.'

Rachel gasped and stared unbelievingly at the inspector.

Aaron spoke with alarm in his voice, 'What are you talking about? How could I have killed him if I was unconscious at the time?'

Didier replied, 'You could have drugged yourself after the act to give yourself an alibi. Besides I merely mentioned that your assistant was dead. Yet you immediately assumed he was murdered? How could you be so sure that he was murdered unless you were involved?'

'That is not fair. You said he was found dead. It was a natural assumption on my part. Healthy young men don't drop dead just like that. I think after all the recent murders that have been unable to solve, you are merely looking for a scapegoat to cover your own inefficiency. Rest assured, Inspector that once again, you are making a wrong arrest. That is all I have to say. I shall not be answering any more questions without the presence of my advocate. Good day to you all!'

Chapter Sixteen

'Of all the nonsensical things I've seen in my life, this takes the cake!' Rachel was livid with the inspector's decision to arrest Aaron Berger and made her views perfectly clear to Jeremy as the two of them exited from the Hospital.

Jeremy responded in his own quiet way that it was best not to interfere in police business and allow the inspector do his job and that perhaps she was allowing her personal friendship with Aaron to cloud her judgement. Rachel fell silent. He suggested that they take their mind off the unpleasant event by taking a taxi to look up the address in Montmartre.

Twenty minutes later they found themselves weaving through dingy lanes and bylanes of Montmartre. Finally the taxi stopped by some train tracks. The driver pointed to a large dilapidated three storeyed building opposite the tracks, which looked like a warehouse, and told them they had arrived. They requested him to wait, got out of the taxi and started walking towards the gate.

The old compound wall was fifteen feet high and had glass shards on top. It was drizzling again and the deserted charcoal grey building looked ominous against a steel grey sky. There was a rusted iron gate that led into the compound but it was secured with heavy metal chains and padlocked. Peering through the gate, Rachel noticed that most of the windows on the ground floor were all boarded up and the glass windows on the first floor were mostly broken. The compound was overgrown with weeds and the walls were covered with patches of moss. There wasn't a soul in sight except for a pie dog who was rummaging through a pile of rubbish at the far end of the compound.

Jeremy clanked the gate and hollered, 'Hello! Bonjour! Anybody there?'

The dog looked up and started wagging his tail and barking in a friendly fashion but apart from that they got no other response.

Jeremy spoke, 'It must be deserted. It certainly looks like it is.'

'Look, Jeremy, there's a signboard over there but I can't make out what it says. It's covered in mud and the letters are faded completely.'

'I wonder why Pierre Lambert gave us an address for a deserted warehouse. He must have had some reason to believe that there was something going on here. But what?'

'Let's walk around the compound wall. There must be a break somewhere.'

'What makes you think that?' Jeremy asked.

'Well the dog got in, didn't he? And he's only a dog not a chimpanzee. He couldn't have possibly scaled such a high compound wall. Come along.'

They started walking. There was a muddy path to one side. It was a large compound with trees and shrubs growing around it and they kept walking through the mud for about five hundred yards till they came across another high compound wall that merged with this one. It looked like it belonged to another building at the back. Although the wall was old and the plaster had crumbled in places, revealing patches of brickwork, it was intact. They had reached a dead end.

Jeremy ventured, 'Perhaps, the dog got in from a break in the wall between these two buildings?'

'Or perhaps the building isn't as deserted as it seems and the watchman's just gone out to get a bite to eat or something.'

Jeremy shrugged his shoulders. 'At any rate I don't think we are going to learn anything useful by hanging about here any longer.'

They trudged back to the taxi. Rachel nodded and plucked some leaves and managed to get some of the clumps of mud off her shoes. Jeremy followed suit. Seeing that it was almost time for lunch, they asked the taxi driver to drop them off at a cafe in Montmartre.

II

When they got back to their hotel, the parlourmaid informed Rachel that a Mrs. Rosenheim had telephoned for her and had requested that she call back as soon as she got in.

She thanked her and as Jeremy took the keys and excused himself to go upstairs and soak in a bath, Rachel headed to the telephone in the foyer to make the call.

Mrs. Rosenheim picked up on the first ring. She had evidently been sitting by her telephone, waiting for her call. 'Rachel, thank goodness you called. I am going mad with worry. Another murder and now Aaron has been arrested. We must do something. Will you accompany me? I'd like to give that Inspector a piece of my mind! Aaron wouldn't hurt a fly.'

Rachel placated her as best as she could and gave her the same advice that Jeremy had given her earlier and told her that the best thing they could do for Aaron was to try and solve this case as quickly as possible. She made her see that causing a commotion would in all probability, make things worse for him.

It took some convincing but Prudence Rosenheim finally came around to her viewpoint and agreed to remain calm. Then almost as an afterthought she said, 'Oh, Rachel, you didn't tell me that your mother was planning to visit. Thank you for giving her this telephone number. You could have knocked me down with a feather when she called some time ago and informed me that she would be in Paris, the day after tomorrow. She said that she would like to visit us. Please do bring her to meet me soon.'

Rachel promised to do so and then hung up. It had almost slipped her mind, amidst the chaos of the past twenty-four hours that she had invited her mother to Paris. She sat in the armchair in the foyer for a few moments lost in thought and then galvanised herself to take action. She left a message for Jeremy that she was going to run some errands and left the hotel.

She smiled to herself as she stepped out on the streets of Paris. She had her shopping list ready in her mind – she was going to buy a pair of black trousers, a black turtleneck sweater, a black balaclava, a pair of gloves with a good grip, a torch, soft rubber soled shoes, a packet of biscuits and a good sturdy length of rope with a grappling hook.

Just as she turned the corner, preoccupied with her thoughts, she collided headlong into a familiar figure. As she lost her balance, the man held her steady, and she realised with chagrin that she had fallen into the arms of Pietro Santinelli.

'So sorry, Madame. I was just coming to meet you and your husband.' The devastatingly attractive smile followed.

She looked back at him steadily as she extricated herself from his embrace and said, 'Well, as you can see, I'm going out. But you can go ahead and meet my husband. You'll find him at the hotel.'

'Perhaps I can walk with you for a bit?'

She was about to politely tell him to go away but then she realised that while she knew where she could get everything else on her shopping list, she hadn't the faintest idea where she could find a grappling hook in Paris and her communication skills in French left a lot to be desired. She spoke. 'Alright, Pietro but only for a bit. And on one condition - that you stop treating me like the rest of the women you know.'

'I am sorry but I do not understand.'

'I'm perfectly sure, you do. No more of that Don Juan nonsense. I am not about to fall for it, capisce?'

His face broke into a wide smile, 'Ah! You speak Italian? Bella!'

She smiled back and said, 'Just a smattering, so don't get too excited. I spent a year in Italy, a long, long time ago. Now, if you are going to walk with me, you might as well make yourself useful. I want you to take me to an iron-monger's, where I can buy a grappling hook.'

'But why does a beautiful woman like you, want a grappling hook?'

Rachel rolled her eyes, 'There, you're doing it again. Just tell me where I can find one!'

He put his hands up in mock surrender, 'Sorry, sorry, I will do just as you say. I am but your slave.'

Rachel groaned inwardly and gave up trying to correct him. She came to the realisation that flirting came as naturally to him as breathing did to most people. And she also realised that she had found the perfect antidote to resist his undeniable charm – in the analysis that she now found his deadly attraction more amusing rather than alluring. She began to feel more relaxed as they walked.

Chapter Seventeen

Rachel asked Pietro, 'So what did you come to see us about?'

'I wanted to ask you, that is, your husband and you, if you could intervene on my behalf. If you could speak to the Inspector regarding Aaron's arrest. I have known Aaron for years and he would never harm anyone let alone murder someone. I am aware that Monsieur Richards has some influence with the Inspector. Perhaps he could speak with him and show him that he has made a terrible mistake.'

Rachel shook her head, 'Believe me, there is nothing I'd like to do better but my husband is convinced that we ought not to interfere in police matters. Between you and me, I too was outraged that the Inspector decided to arrest Aaron in the first place. I felt he had no grounds to. But for some reason, my husband happens to have a very high opinion of Inspector Lachaille's judgement and I happen to have a very high opinion about my husband's judgement. And his mind seems to be made up. So I'm afraid, talking to him won't do you much good.'

'But, what if his judgement is wrong this time? He is a man, not a God.'

'You could try, I did. There's no harm in trying, I suppose,' Rachel shrugged.

They walked a few moments in silence and then Rachel asked him casually, 'I know this may sound like a strange question to you but I have my reasons to ask. What is the nature of your relationship with your brother?'

'My brother? We don't see eye to eye. We never did, even as children. Me – I am a lover and I love life, people and beautiful things. My brother – he likes to control everything; people, money, things. He likes everything to be just so and life is never just so. People are people and they make mistakes. He does not forgive easily.'

'I daresay you both have your differences. I am yet to meet a set of siblings that don't but tell me, why does he think you were behind his wife's murder? Were you and his wife on difficult terms too?'

'No. Sarah enjoyed my company and that made him jealous.'

'Why would he be jealous? Were you lovers?'

Pietro shook his head, 'It was more complicated than that. Their marriage was like that. You won't understand.'

'Try me. Tell me about their complicated marriage. Your brother gave me the impression that his marriage was a happy one.'

'Then he lied. Sarah told me just before she was killed that she was going to file for divorce.'

'Why?'

'She was very unhappy. In the beginning she was in love with him, yes. But she realised soon enough that he did not love her. He is not capable of love. He merely wanted control over her – one of the richest women in the world,' Pietro said and then his eyes turned dreamy as he spoke. 'She was so childlike. A wonderful girl and she was so much like me – a lover of life.'

'Were you two very close?'

'We were very close but not in the way you think. She came to trust me but he hated that. He was insanely jealous of anything and anyone, she paid attention too. She once told me that she was glad that we were not living in medieval times because left to him, he would have kept her locked up in a tower.'

'Good grief, as bad as that?'

'Yes. He would ask her to account for every second of her time, where she was going, who she was with and what she was spending her money on. He made her life intolerable and she accepted it for a while and then when she could no longer bear it, she rebelled. She went to the opposite extreme. She started living life on her own terms. Luckily for her, she had never given him complete control of her money but once she made up her mind that she would no longer allow him to manipulate her, she took back his signing authority. He was so angry but there was nothing he could do about it. So he took it out on her in different ways.'

'What sort of ways?' Rachel was intrigued.

'He started having affairs openly. But when he saw it made no difference to her, he did something much worse.'

Rachel almost thought that Pietro was going to admit that the Count killed his wife in cold blood but his revelation was different.

'He started wooing the one person that she depended upon and loved most in her life - her closest friend and confidant. He wooed this woman with such a vengeance, such tenacity and power that the woman had no choice in the matter. Their affair devastated Sarah. She went into a deep depression.'

'I think I know who you are referring to. But just to be on the safe side, who was this woman?'

He gave a hollow laugh. 'Everyone knows. It's not a secret. It was none other than Viola Chartreuse. Plus she also had money, not as much as Sarah did but it was enough. My brother no longer needed Sarah for anything.

And their marriage crumbled to dust. And Viola – she was and still is, a perfect match for my brother. As cold hearted as a snake. Sarah never recovered from her betrayal.'

'Were they lovers? Sarah and Viola, I mean.'

Pietro laughed scornfully, 'No, you have been listening to idle gossip. Parisians have too much time on their hands so they indulge in it. There is no truth in that.'

'But I saw the painting Isabelle made. She depicted them as lovers.'

'That was just artistic expression. Isabelle told me that was her master stroke and that the depiction gave her painting depth - anyone who saw it would always be in two minds and wonder – were they or weren't they?'

'I see. Was Isabelle a close friend of yours?'

'We were friends but she had too much going on in her head all the time. She would let you come close but no closer. She was a good artist and perhaps if she had lived longer, she may have even become a great artist. When she painted, she went into a different world. I sat for her once and in those eight hours she just painted. I mean it. She did not stop once, not even for a drink of water. It was like she was a spirit without the needs of a physical body.'

'You were out walking with her the night Sarah died. What did you two talk about?'

'She was very different that evening. I met her at Aaron's house. He was having one of his art soirees that evening and she asked me if I would like to take a walk with her. The party was boring anyway so I did. But she was different that night. I sensed that she just wanted to get away and keep walking. She was very angry about something. But I was not sure about what and I had never seen her that way before.'

'You didn't ask?'

'Of course I did but she said it did not concern me. But she did say that she would have to take steps about something soon. It was a cold controlled anger. I don't even know why she wanted me to come along. Most of the time we walked in silence. She was deep in thought over something. She said something about there being too much evil in this world.'

'That sounds ominous. And when you heard the news of her death, did you mention it to the police?'

'Of course I did.'

'Did her death affect you badly?'

'I was shocked of course but I neither loved her nor hated her. She was the kind of person who you could like but in an indifferent way. It is hard to explain.'

Before she could respond, or ask him anything else, Pietro stopped and pointed to a shop with a sign that read *La quincaillerie*. 'You will find what you are looking for here. Just ask for *ancre à jet*.'

Rachel said, 'Thank you. You do seem to know your way around Paris. When did you move here?'

'Four years ago, while the war was in full swing. I was smuggled in, through the border by my brother's friends.'

'That is interesting! Look, it's been a pleasure chatting with you, Pietro, but I do have some more errands to run and I can find my way from here on. If you want to catch my husband, you had better head back to the hotel now.'

He tipped his hat, 'It was a pleasure to be in your company, Madame.'

Rachel smiled back at him. 'Please, call me Rachel. And I am glad you feel this way even though I did end up haranguing you. Once again, thank you for everything. Ciao!' She said gracefully.

'Prego cara!' he responded in Italian and gave her a heart melting smile, as she waved goodbye and stepped into the shop.

Moments later as she was making her purchase, it struck her that she had forgotten to ask him about his disagreement with Sarah, over the Rembrandt, which the Count claimed to have overheard the night before his wife's death. She scanned the street through the shop's windows, to see if he was still there but it was too late. He was already gone.

Chapter Eighteen

Anna Marie Bouvier was at the green grocers in Bobigny. Although food rationing in France had ended just after the war did in 1945, prices had gone up unreasonably since then. Bread was still rationed and there had been a further cut in bread rations earlier in the year. That meant an increase in demand for her homemade leek and chicken pies. Luckily flour was not rationed and she grew leeks and carrots in her garden and got a fair supply of eggs from the chickens in her yard. As she bought the remainder of her supplies, she was thankful that Suzette had left her bread tickets for her. Basket in hand, she left the shop and was passing by the tobacconists' when she chanced upon the latest edition of *Le Parisien Libere*. As her eyes fell on the lower fold of the front page, she gasped.

She recognised the man in the photograph. A newspaper was not a luxury she normally indulged in but she had to know who he was and perhaps it would throw some light on why Suzette had taken Étienne and disappeared. She purchased a copy and walked home as briskly as she could.

Upon reaching home, she entered the kitchen, set her shopping basket on the kitchen table and spread the paper out in front of her. She read and re-read the article twice and even though her hand was shaking she folded the paper carefully and sat lost in thought. Now she was sure that both Suzette and Étienne were in terrible danger. Compared to her, her sister had always been the more courageous one but this time Anna Marie knew instinctively that Suzette had bitten off far more than she could chew.

This time she had somehow gotten mixed up in something far more sinister than Suzette had led her to believe. Half an hour later, Anna Marie had come to a decision. She would take the morning train to Paris and visit Inspector Didier Lachaille. She had liked the man and felt she could trust him. Anyhow she was left with no choice but to confide in him. She had to do something to protect Suzette and Étienne. She got up and rummaged through her kitchen drawers till she found his card. She put it in her handbag.

II

About ten miles away from where Anna Marie was, Rachel was in a public restroom in Montmartre. She had changed into her new black baggy trousers and turtleneck and was in the process of slipping on her rubber soled shoes. She packed her woollen dress and the other items in a cheap travel rucksack she had just bought from a vendor on the street outside. She slipped in the batteries and double checked to see if her new torch was working. She had bought a medium sized one because only those came with a cord that could be hung from the neck. It would be dark outside by the time she reached. She checked the other compartments of the bag to see if everything else was in its place then satisfied with her packing, she stepped out and hailed a taxi.

She gave him the address of the street the warehouse was located on. She had noted during her visit earlier in the day that there were no streetlights but there was a control tower for the railway line opposite the warehouse. She gave a sigh of relief when she saw that the light from the tower provided enough illumination for her to spot the warehouse from a distance of about five hundred yards. The moment it came into view, she asked the driver to stop the taxi and wait there. He didn't look too pleased about it but she gave him a large tip and promised him a much larger one if would wait. He grudgingly agreed. She managed to communicate to him that she would be back, at the most, in half an hour. He nodded.

She walked up to the compound wall of the warehouse and took the muddy path adjacent to it. The sky had cleared and the half moon provided enough light to see by. About twenty feet into the path, she switched on her torch. Up ahead, she saw the tree that she had planned to climb. She switched off her torch, hung it by the cord around her neck. She put on her gloves and her balaclava and put the packet of biscuits in her trouser pocket. If the dog was still there, she hoped that the biscuits would be a sufficiently adequate bribe. Then she took off the new sheepskin jacket, which she had got at a bargain price from the same street vendor she had bought the rucksack from, and tied it around her waist. After that she brought out the rope and the grappling hook and coiled it diagonally across her torso.

She left the rucksack at the foot of the tree and started climbing. It was not as difficult as she had imagined it would be. Parts of the bark that were covered in moss were slippery and she was thankful that both her gloves and her rubber soles had a decent enough grip. Climbing trees had been a hobby when she was a child and she was relieved to find that it was akin to riding a bicycle – despite a large time gap one never quite forgets how to.

Once she was at an arm's length distance from the top of the compound wall, she used her left hand to untie the jacket from her waist and put it over the shards of glass. Two feet higher, she could see over the compound wall. The warehouse was in complete darkness and looked as deserted as it had during the day. She searched for a sliver of light, coming from any of the windows, without any luck. There was no sign of the pie dog either. She fixed the grappling hook to one of the sturdiest branches on the tree and threw the attached rope onto the other side. From here on she would have to rely on her wits as she had no previous experience to rely on.

As she put one foot tentatively over the sheepskin jacket, she could still feel the shards of glass under her shoe. It was no good. They would most certainly go through both the jacket and her rubber soled shoe, if she put her full body weight on it. She took off the jacket and used the bottom of her torch to smash a few shards. It worked. Flattening just enough glass that would fit the space of one shoe, she double folded the jacket over the flattened area and tried once again. Two minutes later she was slipping down the rope on the other side far too quickly for her own comfort and landed on her derriere with a thud. The elation of what she had just done overruled any pain she felt. She could deal with that later. At least she was in!

She took the path of the shadows and moved closer to the main building. She heard a dog barking in the distance. She wasn't sure if the sound was coming from this compound or the next but she didn't want to wait around any longer to find out. She started working fast and tried one boarded window after another. On her third try, she got lucky. One of the loose boards came off as she pulled. Whatever glass had been on the window had been smashed long ago and she managed to squeeze herself through the opening. She was finally inside the building!

Chapter Nineteen

Inside the warehouse, Rachel stood quietly, waiting for her breathing to calm down. She hoped that her eyes would adjust to the darkness but it was no good. The only light that came in, was from the window she had just removed the board from. The rest of the space was pitch black. Touching the wall she moved sideways like a crab till she was about ten feet away from the open window and switched on her torch once again. The balaclava was making her head and face itch, so she took it off and put it in a pocket.

As she shone the light in front of her, she could see that at a distance of about twenty feet, there were wooden crates stacked up with a large tarpaulin over the top. There were smaller crates too. They had stickers of S.S. Argentine stuck on them. She cursed under her breath for not having a bought along a Swiss army knife. How on earth would she get one open to check what was inside? All her careful planning had come to nothing. The only sharp object she had brought with her was stuck to a tree outside on the other side. How could she have been so stupid! She could have kicked herself. And in her despair, she kicked out of habit, felt her foot connect to something hard and heard a piece of metal scraping against the floor. It sounded like music to her ears. Focussing her torch on the floor, she found several metallic implements, probably kept there for the very purpose of opening the crates! Obviously the people who needed to open them legitimately, would need the tools to do so.

She removed the cord from around her neck and kept the torch switched on, on a larger crate next to her and picked up a medium sized wrench and tried to pry open a small crate. There was a loud ripping sound, as the board came away. The way sound magnified and echoed in this large space gave her quite a turn. She pushed away the straw on top and found smaller cardboard boxes. Ripping open the lid of one, she was taken aback. She gently took out the object within – even under the pale beam of the torch, it took her breath away. It was a glittering and beautifully carved wooden box inlaid with ivory. As she opened the lid, a tiny exquisitely dressed ballerina started rotating and the melody of a Viennese waltz began to float about and echo in the desolate hall. She quickly brought the lid down again and the music stopped. Rachel couldn't help but grin and think to herself that she would have made the worst burglar in the history of thievery.

The music box was small enough to fit into her pocket and she kept it. A voice in her head, which sounded a lot like her Sunday school teacher, told her that she was in fact thieving but she told it to be quiet and retorted that she was keeping it as evidence, evidence of what, she was still unclear. She walked over to a larger box and used the wrench to open it. This time she struck gold. There were paintings inside, miniatures but paintings nonetheless.

She looked about and realised that the larger crates could contain much larger canvasses, even sculptures. At least she knew now why Pierre had given her this address. This must be the counterfeiter's den. The place where they stored the fakes. It looked like a large operation alright.

The only thing that surprised her was that it wasn't guarded. It was time to call in the police. She would go directly to La Crim and report her findings. Jeremy would be livid at what she had done, and the risk she had taken, apart from unlawfully breaking and entering – something he would never have condoned or allowed her to do, had she confided in him. But in the end, she was sure that he would come around, to seeing her point of view that there was no other way to get to the bottom of this. At least now, based on her findings, the police could get a search warrant and raid the warehouse.

As she got up from her crouched position, she heard the sound of voices outside and then the clank of the metal chain on the gate. She panicked. The place was guarded after all and whoever was guarding it had just come back. As fear pumped adrenaline through her veins, her mind was frozen but her body took over and before she realised it, she had switched off the torch, run over to the window, which she had come in through and squeezed her way out. Using the shadows, she quickly navigated back to the spot, where she had left the rope hanging. She had no recollection of ever having done any mountain climbing but her body was taking all the decisions and it had decided to climb its way to safety. As she was half way up, she heard the dog barking closer to the gate and this time around, there was nothing remotely friendly about its bark.

She heard two raised male voices and then the sound of the gate creaking open, followed by the sound of running footsteps coming from the front of the building. She put her hand over the compound wall and to her relief, the sheepskin jacket was still there. She lifted her body up and just as was pulling up the rope, the dog came running right up to the compound wall, snarling and barking furiously. Next thing she heard was a gunshot behind her. She literally scrambled down the tree, scraping every piece of exposed skin that she had. Then lifting the rucksack, she ran for her life towards the taxi.

The taxi driver was shouting at her in French, as she jumped in and she closed the door. She shouted back at him, 'Go, go, go!' More sounds of gunshots followed and that was enough for him to get the engine running and the car moving. As he screeched away from the warehouse, the glass behind Rachel's head shattered as another shot was fired at the taxi.

Only when the driver, still shouting and gesticulating at her, brought the car onto one of the main streets in Montmartre, did her breathing start coming back to normal. And that was when she realised that blood was flowing down into the nape of her turtleneck, from the left side of her head. She felt faint. Before she passed out, she managed to tell the driver in broken French to take her to La Crim and ask for Inspector Didier Lachaille. And that was the last thing she remembered.

Chapter Twenty

At ten o'clock in the night, Didier Lachaille joined Jeremy as he paced up and down furiously in the hospital corridor, just outside the room that Rachel had been admitted to.

The inspector spoke, 'We've just released the taxi driver. He gave a statement but he is still waiting for some payments. Apparently, Madame promised him a large one. Plus he wants to know if you will reimburse him for the smashed rear windshield of the taxi.'

'I'll do that and more. It looks like his quick thinking saved her life. If he hadn't driven her back to la Crim...'

'No, that was your wife's quick thinking. It seems she specifically told him to bring her there and gave him my name before she passed out in his taxi.'

'I still think the chap deserves a medal for not deserting her at the warehouse, anyone else in his place would have driven off without a second thought, upon hearing the sound of gunshots. I shudder to think what would have happened to her, had he done that.'

'Yes, your wife did an incredibly foolish thing by trying to take the law into her hands. I have half a mind to arrest her in the morning.'

Jeremy nodded and grumbled, 'Go ahead, it may do her some good! Might even put some sense in her head!' Then as he walked away to meet the heroic taxi driver, Didier's eyes followed his retreating figure with an amused smile.

II

The next morning, Rachel awoke to find herself in a strange room. As she looked around, she noticed a familiar figure with her back towards her, arranging flowers in a vase on a table by the window.

'Mother?' She squeaked. Her voice sounded strange even to her own ears.

Elizabeth Markham turned. 'Darling, you are up!' She looked elegant and aristocratic as always.

'Almost,' Rachel said groggily, as she tried to sit up on her uncomfortable hospital bed but gave up and sank back into the pillows. 'Ow! My head hurts like the Dickens!'

'It would, my dear. The doctor told me that he had to give you stitches on your ear and that he took out some shards of glass from the back of your head. Now, you just lie back and I'll go fetch the nurse and give a shout out to Jeremy. He's gone to fetch some coffee for me.'

Rachel groaned and felt the left side of her head. It was swathed in bandages. No wonder she couldn't hear properly. As her mother reached the door, she said, 'Thank you, Mums.'

'For what, my dear?'

'For coming, darling Mums. Welcome to Paris,' Rachel said with a grin.

Elizabeth smiled back at her daughter and shook her head, 'I've raised an incorrigible child!' And left the room.

Five minutes later, Elizabeth returned with Jeremy in tow. Jeremy had somewhat recovered his sense of humour after fuming and fretting for the most part of the night. He came in and sat by Rachel's bedside and took her hand.

Rachel gave him a wan smile and squeaked, 'Darling, are you still terribly annoyed with me?'

Jeremy smiled at her and said, 'No. God knows I should be. But I'm just glad you are back, safe and partially sound. What were you thinking?'

'I am sorry, darling but I had to find out what was in there. For poor dead Pierre's sake. For Aaron's sake. Oh! That reminds me, did the inspector find the music box? It was in my trouser pocket.'

'Yes, I do believe he mentioned something like that but what has that got to do with any of this?'

'Darling, it has everything to do with it. Don't you see? I pinched it from the warehouse. I actually got inside. And that music box is evidence. I found boxes and boxes of things at the warehouse!'

Elizabeth Markham raised an eyebrow, 'I shouldn't be interrupting and I haven't a clue as to what you're referring to but aren't warehouses supposed to have boxes and boxes of things?'

Jeremy groaned and told Elizabeth, 'And now apart from breaking and entering, they'll have to charge her with burglary as well. Splendid.'

Rachel responded, 'As long as they raid the place and round up those counterfeiting scoundrels that shot at me, they can charge me with whatever they like.'

Elizabeth spoke, 'Rachel! Your father will have a heart attack if he finds out you're about to be charged with burglary! Years of finishing school. An expensive European education and you end up pinching things from warehouses!'

Rachel grinned at her mother. 'You can tell him it's all for a good cause, Mother.'

Elizabeth Markham rolled her eyes as Jeremy laughed.

The doctor came in, followed by a nurse who wheeled in a trolley, rattling with medical equipment and tincture bottles.

Rachel piped up, 'Good morning, Monsieur le Docteur!'

'Bonjour, Madame!' The doctor responded and the young nurse giggled.

Then turning to Jeremy and Elizabeth, the doctor smiled and said, 'The patient looks sufficiently recovered but we will change the dressing before we give the discharge, eh?'

Rachel answered jocularly, 'As long as you give me enough pain medicine to douse an elephant, doctor, I reckon, I'll be just fine.'

The doctor looked at her for a moment and then said in a serious voice, 'Ma foi! You have been very lucky. The wounds are superficial and the bullet merely grazed your ear. Had it been one inch closer you would not be here today, or worse, you may have survived only to live the remainder of your life in a vegetative state. I saw many such cases during the war.'

Rachel's smile faded as she understood the import of his words. She had acted on an adventurous whim and foolishly put herself in danger without thinking twice about her loved ones or her own safety. She glanced at Jeremy and her mother, saw the concern in their eyes and felt a tremendous pang of guilt, followed by an immense wave of gratitude for being spared this time. The doctor was right. Death was not to be feared as much as the indignity of going through life without her faculties intact. For one terrible moment she saw herself in a wheelchair, a blank look in her expressionless eyes, unable to move or clothe or feed herself ever again. The image horrified her. She shuddered inwardly at what might have been. To think that she had taken her innumerable blessings for granted and the audacity with which she had assumed that she would go into that warehouse and come out unscathed suddenly staggered her senses. She had never been overly religious but she promised herself that she would stop by at a church, any church, as soon as she was able to.

The doctor continued, 'Also as this is a police case, I have informed them that you are awake now. They will be here soon to take your statement. Now we will examine the wounds and change the dressing.'

Rachel nodded and as the nurse put a thermometer in Rachel's mouth, Jeremy said, 'We'll be right outside.' He escorted Elizabeth out of the room.

Chapter
Twenty One

Back at La Crim, Didier was surprised to see Anna Marie Bouvier waiting for him when he walked through the main hall at nine in the morning. She got up from her chair and smiled as he came in. She looked so different that for a second back there he almost didn't recognise her. She was neatly dressed, her shoulder length hair framed her face in flattering waves and she had put on some lipstick. She looked prettier today and younger somehow. He tipped his hat at her and asked her to give him a few minutes, so he could settle down and go through the day's agenda and assign certain tasks to his team. That way he would be able to give her his complete attention.

She nodded and sat down again. As he went up the stairs, he noticed that she had taken out a folded newspaper from her travel bag and occupied herself with reading it. There was something very pleasant and peaceful about the woman. He smiled to himself as he set about his daily routine on entering his office. Ten minutes later, he asked the gendarme to bring her in.

She stepped into his large and well appointed office and looked about with unadulterated awe. Then she walked up to his desk and shyly took out a parcel for him. She told him it was just a little something she had baked last night for his wife and family.

He accepted it with gratitude and informed her that he was a bachelor and that he had really enjoyed the pie the other day and that he was sure he would cherish this treat aswell. He motioned her to take the chair in front of him and tell him what had brought her to La Crim. He asked if she had finally received the much awaited post card from her sister.

She shook her head as she sat in the visitor's chair and brought out the newspaper from her handbag once more. She pointed to the picture of the murdered man and informed Didier in her no nonsense way that she had recognised him as the man who had paid her sister a visit, on that fateful day. And that she feared for her sister's safety. She beseeched him to help and protect both Suzette and Étienne – the little boy. She said that she now realised that they were in very real danger and were in all probability, running from the same person or persons who had murdered Pierre Lambert.

Didier nodded and said it was quite possible. But what could he do? His hands were tied and he couldn't protect Suzette or the child if he didn't know where they were.

That was when she looked down at her hands and told him in a small voice that she had not been completely truthful with him the other day. And that she had given her sister a solemn promise that she would not reveal her or Étienne's whereabouts to anyone. But after what had happened she knew that even God would forgive her for breaking such a promise.

Didier said nothing.

She told him that they were in a small village in Dordogne, about sixteen miles from Lalinde, where her uncle had a farm but then a lot of artists knew about the place. Alexandre Dubois himself had taken a group of artists to stay at the farmstead and paint for a few months, the past summer. Anna Marie thought they would be safe there but after learning about Pierre's murder, she had realised that if the killers were part of the same artistic circle, or in touch with any of the artists, they would probably be able to figure out where Suzette was. And that they could hunt her down with ease on that lonely farm and no one would know a thing for days. The nearest neighbours were at least three miles away.

Didier pushed a pen and paper across the desk towards her asked her to write down her uncle's name and the name of the village.

As she wrote, he reassured her that she had done the right thing by coming to him now, and that he would personally see to it that Suzette and Étienne were given a safe escort back to Paris, as soon as possible.

Before she left, Didier asked her if she knew who Étienne's father was. She shook her head. All she knew was what Suzette had once mentioned in passing, on a day when Étienne was throwing a childish tantrum - that he had inherited his father's Italian genes.

II

In another room at la Crim, an art expert was examining the music box. He took off the eyeglass and addressed Henri Beauchamp in French.

'It is one of the finest pieces I have seen and in excellent condition. Early 19th century. And there is an inscription under the lid that is very faint but I can make barely make out the date as 1837. This ought to be in a museum. I am not sure but I think this may be Antonie Farve's work.'

'So this is not a fake?'

'Certainly not! It is clearly of Swiss origin, as I said I cannot make out the inscription, it has faded and there is a patina of time over it. Where did you find it?'

'It is part of a case we are investigating. Can you give me a rough valuation of this piece?'

The art expert did and Henri Beauchamp whistled under his breath, 'As much as that?'

'Perhaps more, far more, if it turns out to be a genuine Farve!'

III

After taking Rachel's statement at the hospital, a team of gendarmes led by Inspector Beauchamp reached the warehouse at Montmartre.

They had a search warrant and they broke the padlock on the gate. Beauchamp walked to the big wooden door of the warehouse building and noticed that it was ajar. That seemed suspicious after all that Rachel had told him and he took out his revolver from the holster and entered. The hall was dark and the windows were all boarded up except for the third one on the right just as Rachel had described. But there was nothing else in the hall. Nothing. The crates were gone. There was no indication that they had ever been there. As he walked in further his foot hit a metallic object. He picked it up. It was a wrench.

Wrench in hand, he gave orders to the gendarmes to check the entire building. They split up into two groups and went up to check the second and third floors. But Beauchamp was sure that they would find nothing. The goods had been moved overnight and if it hadn't been for the antique music box purportedly taken from this warehouse and Rachel Markham's statement of her findings, there would have been no proof that the crates had ever been there. Rachel had been right in assuming that there was something sinister going on.

The warehouse had been leased to a KM trading company. He would be receiving the files from the Directorate of Companies shortly. He wondered if the organisation even existed. There had been several instances of fictitious documentation being used to lease out buildings. And especially after the war, there was an economic slump, businesses had slowed down, and owners often gave out leases without due diligence, as long as payments were being made on time. He headed back to la Crim to share his findings with Didier Lachaille.

Chapter Twenty Two

At the hospital, Rachel had been given a strict warning directly from Didier that although he was prepared to grant her leniency in this particular incident, given the circumstances that her actions were based on the best of intentions, he told her quite categorically that he would not think twice before arresting her if she broke the laws of the land a second time. Rachel had given him her word that there would be no repeat offence from her end. Inwardly she knew that she had no intention of risking life and limb irrespective of the temptations born out of curiosity. She felt she had learnt her lesson for good.

After being discharged from the hospital, Jeremy hailed a taxi. As the taxi passed through the streets of Paris, she asked Jeremy if they could stop at a Church on the way to their hotel.

He raised an eyebrow but made no comment. He gave the driver instructions and within ten minutes the three of them were entering a beautiful Catholic church on Rue Saint-Louis. Rachel lit a candle and then walked over to the altar, where she got down on her knees, closed her eyes and sent up a prayer of gratitude from her soul.

Elizabeth and Jeremy gave her the privacy she needed and spent some time walking around, admiring the gilded interiors. A few minutes later, Rachel joined them. She looked subdued. As Jeremy took her hand, he said softly to her, 'I know that this experience has shaken you, my darling and rightly so, but I want you to know, as a friend, and as someone who has worked in dangerous situations for the better part of my adult life that you must never allow fear to win. Don't permit the fear of what could've happened to change the person you are.'

It took a moment for Rachel to let his words sink in and then she looked at him with complete understanding and said, 'Thank you. I think I needed to hear that.'

Back at the hotel after a light meal, Jeremy and Rachel brought Elizabeth Markham up to date on their findings so far, in the case.

Elizabeth heard them out and finally said, 'All this is most interesting but what is it, that you want me to do?'

Rachel responded without batting an eyelash, 'I want you to pose as a wealthy art buyer who is in the market for a master. You can use your own genuine persona so we don't have to mess about with theatrical nonsense such as fake names or disguises and so forth. Luckily for us, you fit the part so beautifully. If they do decide to run a background check, they will find out that you are in fact wealthy and that you do have a stately home in England to furnish.'

'And?' Elizabeth asked.

'And we, that is, Jeremy and I, and hopefully Mrs. Rosenheim will spread the word around that you are in Paris and that you're interested in investing, preferably, in a Rembrandt or a Vermeer. We'll be at a huge advantage and far closer to solving the murders, if we can get in through the front door of this counterfeiting business. We need to know who makes the offer, and who the mastermind behind this outfit is, and how they transact. Most importantly once you get a viewing, we can sneak in a genuine art expert to examine the painting and then we'll have them cornered.'

Elizabeth nodded contemplatively. 'I see.'

'Look, Mums, I realise that we are dealing with very dangerous people here – dangerous to the point of being completely ruthless, a fact that came to me forcefully and with blinding clarity last night, and if you choose not to do this, I will completely understand.'

Elizabeth bristled. 'My dear girl, where do you think you get your recklessness from? Certainly not from your father – he is far too principled for that sort of thing, with all his army training and discipline. And if those ruffians think they can get away with taking pot shots at my daughter, they had better think again. I'm up for whatever it is, you have planned for me, my darling.'

Rachel looked at her mother with unadulterated admiration and said, 'Bravo, Mums!'

Jeremy smiled at the mother-daughter duo and said, 'Before you two lovely ladies start hatching devious plots, I would like to take a moment here, to say that whatever plan you come up with, this time we are going to keep both Didier & Henri informed well in advance. We are all playing for the same side and I will not have either of you ladies risking your necks without proper police backup.' Then turning to Rachel, he said, 'And darling, while we're on the subject, I managed to nip out this morning and get an early Christmas present for you. I hope you like it.'

He walked over to the bureau and took out a wooden box.

'Does that mean I shan't be getting the ugly Japanese warrior this year?' Rachel grinned.

Jeremy replied with a straight face as he walked over to Rachel. 'Afraid he's already taken, darling and the Count may not be too keen to part with him. Besides, the police have him stored in the evidence room at la Crim, ever since the chap's sword was charged with murder, so you'll just have to make do with this instead, my love.' He bent down to kiss her cheek, as he put the box in her hand.

Rachel opened the lid and gasped. 'Why, it's a pistol. How romantic!'

Elizabeth rolled her eyes, 'Yes, just the thing every girl dreams of. Really, Jeremy!'

Jeremy spoke, 'To be honest Elizabeth, I thought of getting her a bracelet from Cartier but under the prevailing circumstances, I felt this was far more apt.'

Rachel answered without taking her eye off of her new toy, 'Why, Mums, it's the most beautiful thing I've ever seen.' She lifted her present gingerly out of the box and said, 'And it's such a pretty pistol. Just look at all that gorgeous carving. Is that ivory on the handle?'

Jeremy nodded, 'Yes, it is and darling that's technically a revolver, not a pistol. A revolver has six firing chambers whereas a pistol requires reloading after each shot. Now that you own one you may as well acquaint yourself with the technicalities. What you are holding is a Colt 380, hammerless, semi automatic with a safety grip and...'

Rachel interrupted him, 'Oh, Jeremy never mind all that mumbo jumbo. Just teach me how to shoot it!'

Her eyes were shining and Jeremy smiled at her. He was happy to see that his wife was back to being her old cheerful self after her traumatic brush with what might have been.

Chapter Twenty Three

Rachel got up from the metal chair as Aaron Berger was brought into the visitor's room from the lock-up. He smiled at her and said, 'I would have liked to take your hand in mine, ma cherie but as you can see, at the moment they are literally tied.' He lifted his hands in front of him and shook his handcuffs.

'I am sorry, Aaron,' Rachel said and asked the gendarme in broken French if they were necessary.

The gendarme nodded curtly and asked Aaron to take a chair opposite her. As Aaron sat down, the gendarme moved back but stood on guard watchfully.

Aaron looked dishevelled and tired. He sighed as he looked at Rachel. 'They have raided my gallery and my home and found nothing. So they content themselves by interrogating me like the Gestapo.'

Rachel furrowed her brows and asked, 'What are they looking for?'

He replied, 'I don't know, a motive perhaps? Or anything that will link me to the crime, which they have arrested me for. But never mind me, ma cherie, you look as though you got hit by a truck.'

'So I did, in a manner of speaking. Fell down the stairs. A small accident, that is all. But I thought my hat hid most of the damage,' Rachel said, as she adjusted it over her left ear. She had no intention of telling him the real story. She did not know if he could be trusted.

'A difference in opinion with your husband, perhaps?'

'Good Lord, certainly not! Jeremy would be horrified that the thought even crossed your mind.'

'A thousand apologies, Madame. I did not mean to cause offence.'

'None taken. As it is, I've come to ask for your help, so I hope that under the circumstances you would not be offended.'

'Not at all. How can I help?'

'My mother – Lady Elizabeth Markham arrived in Paris yesterday morning with an express wish to buy a painting and since you are the undoubted expert on the subject, it is unfortunate that she cannot meet you but I thought that perhaps you could guide us in some way...'

'Je suis désolé! Your mother is here and I am stuck in this God forsaken situation. What terrible timing. It would have given me immense pleasure to show her around my gallery but perhaps she can visit some other galleries?'

'I doubt that she will find what she is looking for. You see, she is only interested in investing in a master, preferably a Rembrandt or a Vermeer. It is for her home in England – Rutherford Hall.'

'I see. And she already has an art collection?'

'Rutherford Hall does, a pretty decent one at that. It is listed in "England's historic homes and gardens to visit" guide book. People come in busloads over weekends and pay an entry fee to have a walk through.'

'In that case I may be able to help. Do you have a pen and paper?'

Rachel rummaged through her handbag and brought out her telephone directory and proceeded to tear out a sheet of paper. 'This will have to do, I'm afraid.'

'Note down this address.'

Rachel did as he dictated it out. And then asked, 'Rue de l'Abreuvoir in Montmartre – that rings a bell. Is this your home address?'

'Yes.' Then throwing a furtive glance at the gendarme on duty, he leaned forward and spoke in a low voice. 'Take your mother with you. When you get there, ask for Marie Thérèse. She is my housekeeper but she also takes care of the artwork in my personal collection. Tell her I sent you and that I asked her to show you *le nouveau bijou* in my study. It is the latest addition to my collection. She will know what to do.'

'And then?'

'Then ma cherie, once you both have seen it and if your mother likes it, we can discuss terms. Although I have no doubt that if she has a discerning eye, she will immediately realise that it is in fact a jewel, a rare find and look no further.'

'I am indeed grateful. There is just one more thing.'

'Yes?'

'She has a friend with her. May we take him along? You see, she never makes a decision on investing in artwork without his go ahead.'

'Is he also from England?'

'But of course!'

Aaron shrugged his shoulders. 'I have no objection whatsoever. But perhaps your mother and you ought to see the painting by yourselves first and in the event that you do choose to acquire it, you can always get her friend to give you a second opinion, although I very much doubt that will be necessary. It is one of the finest pieces to have entered my collection in the past year.'

II

Rachel stopped by at her hotel to pick up her mother. Elizabeth Markham was ready and waiting for her. They were supposed to visit the Rosenheims for lunch. Rachel informed her that they would need to make a quick detour to Montmartre before visiting the Rosenheims.

'Why are we going to Montmartre?' Elizabeth asked, as Rachel hailed a taxi.

'Because, I've got us a viewing of a painting that you're supposed to be allegedly interested in and it's at Aaron's home in Montmartre.'

'That was quick. I thought you said it might take days to get a viewing.'

'Luckily, it didn't. I just met Aaron and he gave us an immediate offer to view a painting in his collection. As I thought, once I brought you and Rutherford Hall into our conversation, it turned out to be a pretty compelling bait for an art dealer. I think we ought to take him up on his offer and go and see it immediately. We don't want to wait around, just in case he changes his mind, or gets wind of our real motives.'

'But, didn't you want to take an art expert along?'

'Mums, we can do that later. Let's just see what he has on offer. I'm hoping it will be the same Rembrandt that he was trying to sell to the Countess. If it is, I'm hoping it may give us some sort of a clue. Don't ask me what. I'm not so clear about it myself.'

'What are we waiting for then?' Elizabeth asked, as a taxi came to a halt at the curb.

In twenty minutes they were standing at Aaron's front door, on Rue de l'Abreuvoir. They heard the bell chime in the interior and the door was opened by a parlourmaid.

'Oui, Madame?'

Rachel explained that Monsieur Berger had asked them to meet Marie Thérèse and gave the maid her visiting card.

They were shown in to the sitting room and within five minutes, a dignified grey haired lady in her 60s came in. She was dressed in a severe black dress with a white lace collar. She introduced herself as Marie Thérèse and asked them if she could be of any help.

Rachel nodded and explained the circumstances behind their visit and told her that Aaron had asked them to come over for a viewing of a special painting in his study.

Marie Thérèse shook her head and apologised sweetly in French that without any written directions from him, she could not allow anyone into his study.

Then Rachel remembered that he had specifically asked her to use the words *"le nouveau bijou"*. She rephrased her request to include the phrase and immediately the housekeeper's attitude changed. Rachel realised that it must have been some sort of a pre-chosen pass code.

Marie Thérèse smiled and asked the ladies to follow her. They walked through the house and Rachel was impressed. The house in itself was beautiful and the plush interiors were a glowing testimony to Aaron's refined tastes. Most of the rooms they passed on the ground floor were well proportioned and had large French windows with an uninterrupted view of the luxurious back garden. The generous windows allowed natural sunlight to stream into the house and spray the interiors with a golden hue.

They followed the housekeeper through the passageway and up the wooden staircase, into a pentagonal oak panelled study, furnished in contrasting leather and gold. Rachel saw at a glance that this room alone contained a fortune in artwork. She spotted a Cezanne on one of the panels, and a Monet and a Chagall on two others. As she turned around in wonder, she also saw a Gauguin and a Picasso. Her head was spinning. These did not look like forgeries even to her untrained eyes. Aaron had been right. Genuine masters had a magnificent presence of their own. She had seen copies of these paintings before but there was an aura of beauty, history and power which emanated from the original paintings that simply took one's breath away.

Marie Thérèse asked them to wait as she stepped behind the large polished teak desk and took out a bunch of keys. Then she walked over to the side of the room, where a black Chinese lacquer screen, hand painted with golden dragons on it, had been placed. She stepped behind it. They heard the sound of a key turning in its lock. Moments later, she came back with a gilt framed painting and placed it with reverence on a viewing easel in front of a window to their right.

Both mother and daughter gasped in awe.

Elizabeth asked Rachel in a hushed voice, 'Is it a Rembrandt?'

'No, Mums,' she said with genuine reverence. 'This is a Vermeer.'

III

Half an hour later they were at the Rosenheims. As Elizabeth and Prudence embraced each other warmly and sat down to catch up on the lost years of their friendship, Rachel decided to give them some privacy. She excused herself and said she would like to get some fresh air before lunch and take a small walk in the courtyard below.

Ten minutes later she was seated on a stone bench in the courtyard and couldn't shake off the feeling that in chasing a ring of counterfeiters, they were somehow barking up the wrong tree. She was quite sure that the paintings she had seen at Aaron's were original. And that if she had taken an art expert along to examine them, he would have come to the same conclusion. Her mind was in disarray. And yet behind all the confusion in her mind, a small voice kept saying that the paintings were linked to the crimes, somehow. But how? Her mind went to the

Vermeer she had just seen and she realised that she had seen something exactly like that, not so long ago. Perhaps a copy or even a print at a cafe or someplace but for the life of her, she couldn't remember where.

Then her mind went to the sequence of events since their arrival at Paris, Aaron's arrest, her meeting with Pietro followed by her adventure at the warehouse. She made a note to ask Jeremy if Pietro had in fact met him after dropping her off at la quincaillerie the other day. Jeremy had never mentioned it but he may have met him and forgotten to tell her, owing to the series of events that had followed. Her thoughts went to the victims – Countess Santinelli, Isabelle Rosenheim and Pierre Lambert. Their deaths were connected but the link still eluded her. She thought of her last visit here, at the Rosenheim's. Her mind went to Pierre Lambert and she remembered the events of the day at Isabelle's Shiva. How Pietro had come up to her and later, how she had observed Pierre Lambert staring at the mantelpiece with a look of horror frozen on his face.

And that was when it hit her. Suddenly the fog had lifted and she could see clearly. She cursed herself inwardly, 'That's it! I've been a blind bloody bat! I've been so stupid that I could kick myself!' She jumped up and ran to the foyer. The elevator was travelling and she was too impatient to wait. She took the stairs two at a time and ran up to the Rosenheim's apartment. As the door opened, she rushed past the startled butler and ran straight towards the mantelpiece. Both Elizabeth and Prudence stared at her astonished, as she declared loudly to herself, 'I was right! This is what Pierre was looking at. This is where I saw it!'

Then turning to the ladies, she said, 'Mums, please come over here. I'd like you to take a look at this picture and tell me what you see.'

Elizabeth Markham got up and walked over to the mantelpiece. She looked at the picture and said, 'Why, that's a wonderful picture of your family, Pru.'

Rachel spoke impatiently and said, 'Mums, look closer! What do you see behind the grand piano?'

Elizabeth's eyes opened wide as she exclaimed, 'Oh my! It's that Vermeer we just saw.' Then turning to Prudence she asked, 'Pru, was this painting original, the one behind Jonathan's head?'

'Of course it was. It had been in Jonathan's family for generations! Why do you ask?'

Elizabeth exclaimed, 'Rachel darling, you have him now. That man Aaron is obviously dealing in counterfeit art! You don't need an art expert anymore!'

Rachel responded, her eyes far away, 'No, Mums, you have it the other way round. The painting we saw at Aaron's place was the same one in this photograph. And don't you see? We are not dealing with a ring of counterfeiters but something entirely different here. We are dealing with a group of ruthless Nazi's who got away with stolen art during the war! I must give Didier a call.' Turning to Prudence, she asked, 'May I use your telephone?'

Chapter Twenty Four

At la Crim, Henri Beauchamp and Jeremy were in conference with Didier Lachaille and two officers from the Commission de Récupération Artistique. They were introduced to Jeremy as a team of elite officers from different allied nations whose job was restitution of stolen art during the Nazi occupation.

One of the officers who had been introduced as Sous-lieutenant, Jean Paul spoke addressing Jeremy. 'It looks as though your wife may have unwittingly stumbled upon stolen Nazi loot when she broke into the warehouse.'

Jeremy raised an eyebrow, 'Are you serious?'

Henri responded, 'As soon as the expert gave his verdict on the music box, we knew we were dealing with stolen property. And then when we got word from your wife, an hour ago, about the Vermeer, we put two and two together.'

Didier nodded and said, 'I immediately telephoned the curator of Galerie nationale du Jeu de Paume, which was a sorting house for stolen artwork during the occupation and we were was asked to get in touch with Commission de Récupération Artistique, also a part of the group known in America as the Monuments Men.'

'Wait a minute. You told me that was in regard to Aaron Berger's collection. Are you implying that the warehouse too, was filled with treasures robbed from the Jews?' Jeremy asked.

Sous-lieutenant Jean Paul spoke, 'Yes. There is a high possibility of that being the case. You see, during the war, the Nazi's robbed every valuable piece of art, among other things that they could lay their hands upon. Most of the artwork robbed from the Jews went through Jeu de Paume. They viewed the museum as their personal art gallery, where they could just walk in and choose any piece of art that took their fancy. Several officers did so, Hermann Göring being the most notable one. Most of the really valuable pieces were robbed from wealthy Jewish private collectors such as the Bernheims, the Rothschilds, among others. They also seized entire collections worth millions from the notable Jewish art dealers, Paul Rosenberg's collection included. With the help of the resistance, much of the stolen artwork was restored to their rightful owners, however, there are thousands of untraceable stolen masterpieces still at large. We know that many were destroyed but we also have information that many left the country and are still in the hands of the Nazis who evaded justice.'

'So what you are telling us, is that it is not merely a counterfeiting operation that we're up against but something much worse.'

The other officer from Monuments Men, Lieutenant Harding from America, spoke. 'Yes. That just about sums it up.'

Jeremy whistled under his breath.

Didier spoke. 'We also ran a check on the KM trading company. As we suspected, it is a false front. They gave fake documentation to get the lease on the warehouse. By the way, your wife is on her way here from the Rosenheim residence.'

Lieutenant Harding spoke up. 'Apart from checking on Berger's Art collection, we need to enlist your wife's help to find those missing crates. They couldn't have gotten very far but time is of the essence. We must speak to her.'

Jeremy nodded. 'Be my guest. I'm sure she'll be pleased as punch to help with such a noble cause. Only trouble is that like the rest of us in the room, she's probably just as clueless as to where they may have shifted the crates to.'

At that moment, the door opened and the gendarme showed Rachel in.

'I hope I'm not too late, Inspector?' she asked in a slightly breathless voice. 'I came as soon as I could.'

Didier introduced her to the officers and they brought her up to date on their suspicions around the goods she had come across in the dubious KM Trading Company's warehouse.

Rachel thought for a moment and spoke. 'The company may be a fake one but why don't you start by checking shipping records? Every single one of the crates that I spotted, had the S.S. Argentine label on it. Perhaps that will lead us somewhere.'

Lieutenant Harding nodded, 'That is an intelligent suggestion, Ma'am. We'll do that. It is widely known that close to nine thousand Nazi war criminals evaded justice along with stolen treasures and many have found refuge in South America, primarily Argentina. It gives me hope that we are on the right track.'

Rachel's eyes opened wide. 'Why, that is a staggering number, Lieutenant Harding. Well, at least we have some satisfaction in the knowledge that some of the worst Nazi war criminals were tried and convicted at the Nuremberg trials last year.

Lieutenant Harding shook his head. 'Unfortunately there are still many, some even worse than the ones that were tried, who seem to have disappeared into thin air, Franz Stangl and Adolf Eichmann, for example and even more notorious, Josef Mengele, better known as the Angel of Death for his heinous medical experiments conducted on living victims, most of them young children. It will take the world a very long time to recover from such unimaginable horrors inflicted by man upon man. Meanwhile, we will try our best to do the job that we've pledged to do ma'am - and that is to return to people what was once rightfully theirs, a missing part of their history, their home and their culture. Is there anything else that you can think of that may help us?'

Well, not at the moment, Lieutenant. Jeremy, what about you?' She asked, turning towards her husband.

Jeremy responded, 'Well, I suggest you keep an eye on that Friedrich von Schmidt character. I'll eat my hat if it turns out, he's not involved in this, in one way or the other. One of you may want to check on the provenance of his alleged private art collection too. Apparently he houses it in Austria and Switzerland and we suspect that he disposes some of the paintings from time to time through the Berger Art Galerie, here in Paris.'

Didier looked up and spoke slowly as though he had just seen the light. 'Yes, tout à fait! That is probably why Berger refused to divulge the name of his supplier even after being faced with a murder charge. And it was Berger's assistant who pointed you towards the warehouse in the first place. He found out what he had done and killed him. There! We finally have a rock solid motive for Pierre Lambert's murder now.'

II

When Rachel got back to the hotel, Elizabeth Markham informed her that a large bouquet had just been delivered for her with a get well soon card from Count Santinelli, and an invitation to tea, from Madame Chartreuse.

'That is kind of them.'

'I asked the maid to put the flowers in a vase, in your room.'

'Thank you, Mums.'

'What's the matter, darling? You look worried about something.'

'Yes, I am,' Rachel replied and proceeded to tell her mother about their meeting with the Monuments Men officers at la Crim.

Elizabeth listened and when Rachel had finished talking she asked, 'But that's good news. You are finally getting to the bottom of this case.'

'I know, that is what it seems like but there's something wrong and I can't quite put my finger on it but there's something... it's all too pat, somehow. '

'Oh, darling, sometimes the simple solutions turn out to be the right ones.'

'Yes, Mums but not in this case. There's something else going on and I just wish Aaron wasn't so pig headed about disclosing who had telephoned him that evening, at the gallery. Makes me wonder, who he's trying to protect. And even if stolen Nazi artwork is at the root of this, why was the Countess murdered and by whom?'

'Perhaps she found out that he was dealing with the Nazis and threatened to disclose it to the authorities? And perhaps Pru's daughter was murdered for the same reason. It all seems to fit.'

'Yes, like a glove. But something tells me there's more to these murders and I don't think Aaron killed three people to hide the fact that he was dealing with stolen artwork.'

'To my mind, people have killed for far less. After all, his reputation and millions were at stake. Could it be that your fondness for this man Aaron, is the reason you feel this way?'

'Now you sound just like Jeremy. He suggested the same thing when I was angry about the fact that they arrested Aaron without any solid evidence.'

'Jeremy could be right, you know.'

And Rachel found herself echoing Pietro's words, 'He could be wrong too, Mums. After all, he's just a man, not God.'

Chapter Twenty Five

Didier was at his desk trying to make a telephone call. After a few frustratingly futile attempts he finally managed to get through to the police station at Lalinde in Dordogne. Amidst the sudden developments in the case, he had not forgotten his promise to Anna Marie. He spoke to the man on duty and gave him the address of the farmstead in Limeuil, followed by careful instructions for the safe return of both Suzette and Étienne.

Then he sat back and started thinking. There were too many things going on. Berger was the most obvious choice for Pierre Lambert's murder but he had an alibi for the time of the Countess' murder. He was hosting a soiree when she was killed and by all accounts, he never left it. He obviously had an accomplice who did the job for him. Didier wondered if Pietro fit the bill. Strange that the girl who had provided Pietro with an alibi was murdered the same way soon after. Why was she murdered?

Something was missing somewhere and perhaps the answer lay in the girl, Isabelle's death. Was she killed because she threatened to go back on the alibi she had provided? Or was she killed by someone who knew that suspicion would fall on Pietro if she was killed. Where did Suzette fit in all of this? Who had given her a payout and why? There were too many unanswered questions and too much confusion. If only he could see through the darkness.

He decided that while he awaited Suzette's return and with it, hopefully answers to some of the questions, in the meantime he would confront Berger about the allegedly stolen artwork the man was peddling.

As he got up to leave his office, the telephone at his desk rang. It was Lieutenant Harding and he informed Didier that they would need a search warrant to go through Berger's art collection at his residence. So far, they had found nothing incriminating at the Berger Art Galerie.

Didier agreed to send his gendarmes so that they could search the residence under the guise that they were looking for further evidence in the murder case. He asked Harding if there was any way of knowing for sure that the paintings were in fact stolen by the Nazis.

Lieutenant Harding replied in the affirmative. He informed him that the paintings would have markings on the back – the same alpha numerical marking that the Nazis had meticulously used to catalogue paintings stolen from various wealthy Jewish families, was now being used against them to prove their original provenance. Other than that the famous paintings, such as the Vermeer which Rachel Markham had seen, were easily identifiable and catalogued as 'missing in the war' by their team.

Didier thought to himself, 'No wonder the Seurat and Courbet were removed from the public gallery on the same night.' But it also made him wonder who was behind their removal since Aaron Berger's assistant was dead by that time, and Berger himself had been in a drugged state, and could not have ordered their removal.

II

Rachel arrived in time for tea at Madame Chartreuse's apartment, which was situated in an elegant corner of Paris, at Rue de Rivoli, overlooking the Jardin des Tuileries. The sitting room was luxuriously appointed, to the point of being extravagantly so. Madame Chartreuse by contrast was dressed in a simple yet stylish cream suit. She greeted Rachel warmly as if they were old friends and Rachel couldn't help but notice with a tinge of envy that as always, she had an air of effortless chic about her that she had seen in so many women in Paris.

'I do hope you are feeling better now, Madame.'

'Thank you, yes. Please call me Rachel.'

'Well, Rachel, when Tristan informed me that you were in the hospital, I wanted to visit you there but when I telephoned, I was told that you were already discharged.'

'Yes, I had a nasty cut on my ear but luckily not much else.'

'It is good to see you looking so well.'

As they took their seats near the window, Rachel commented on the view.

'Yes, my late husband used this place as his temporary residence whenever he conducted business in Paris. I only moved here after his passing but I like it here. It is in the heart of the city. All my friends live close by. It got very lonely living on our family estate in Compiègne, although it is not too far from Paris. I still keep the house there running on minimal staff through winter, but in summer I move back there, as it is a fine place to entertain guests.'

'I can imagine. I hear that you have a beautiful estate.'

'Yes we have close to forty five acres and the house itself has fourteen bedrooms, stables and a six car garage. Far too large for my needs presently.'

Rachel nodded in agreement and then as their tea was served, she said, 'I missed seeing you at the Berger Galerie the other night.'

'Yes, I had another social engagement to attend but I heard the terrible news soon after it occurred. Tristan telephoned me. And isn't it awful that they arrested Aaron?'

'Yes but I'm sure that the Inspector must have had his reasons', Rachel told her diplomatically, suppressing the urge to inform her about having found stolen art in his study.

'Any idea what those reasons may be? One hears that your husband is closely associated with the police', she asked, in a confidential tone.

'I'm afraid, my husband does not discuss police matters with me.'

'Ah, yes, husbands, they place so little trust in us. It is a pity. Mine kept a mistress hidden from me for fifteen years. Only on his passing did I learn about her when I had to pay death duties for a house in Cap Ferrat that I never knew existed!'

'Are death duties very heavy in France as well?'

'They will be the death of us, this "droits de succession". It is terrible the way the Government takes money from widows. First you lose a husband, and then you lose any benefit you may have gained, from losing a husband', she said cynically.

Rachel laughed, 'At least you are dreadfully honest about it, I'll give you that.'

'Sadly, honesty has always been my Achilles' heel. I have lost close friends because of that.'

'Was the Countess one of them?' Rachel asked candidly.

'Sadly, yes.'

'Because she found out about your liaison with the Count?'

'L'enfant terrible! Who has been filling your ears? Tristan and I have always been friends!'

'But one hears...'

'Hears what and from whom?'

'I know I may get into trouble for this but Pietro told me that...'

Madame Chartreuse interrupted her, 'Pietro is the most awful liar. Please don't listen to anything he has to say. The Count is a fine and upright man. He fought with the Resistance. And that Pietro owes his life to him. But that boy, he is a bad one. I heard that he even got some poor girl into trouble and never took responsibility. Tristan had to settle the matter quietly. He is always paying for Pietro's mistakes.'

'I see.' Rachel took a sip of her tea and continued, 'If I may ask, what was it then that created the rift between you and the Countess?'

'We had a misunderstanding, a trivial argument over a silly painting and she was so young. But for someone so young, she had a big ego. So big that when Tristan tried to intervene she got furious with him and behaved very high-handedly. She tried to use her wealth to put him in his place.'

'Yes, Pietro mentioned that she withdrew his signing authority. But tell me is it true that their marriage was an unhappy one?'

'My dear, no marriage is ever a happy one. There are just different degrees of disillusionment. Some more so than others.'

Rachel shrugged, 'Even so, I just wondered if there is any truth in what he told me.'

'And what was that?'

'That she was about to file for a divorce just before she was killed.'

'I do not know, but I know this - the Count is Catholic and he would have never agreed to a divorce. Besides, she had no grounds for one.'

Chapter
Twenty Six

Rachel, Jeremy and Elizabeth sat together in Elizabeth's room and discussed the case. They had just finished their dinner and were now seated in front of the fireplace with a glass of red wine each.

Rachel told them about her interview with Pietro and her contrasting chat with Viola Chartreuse.

'I just don't know whom to believe. One of them is lying through their teeth and I'll be dashed if I can figure out which one.'

'Just a moment, you mentioned that Pietro wanted to see me.'

'Yes. He said he wanted to ask you if you could intervene on Aaron's behalf. He seemed quite keen on meeting you.'

'Strange, he never showed up here. The last time I saw him, was at the art gallery.'

Elizabeth spoke, 'Interesting, don't you think?'

'Is it?' Rachel asked.

Jeremy responded, 'Your mother is right. Has it occurred to you that he may have singled you out for the express purpose of giving you some cock and bull account of his version of events?'

Rachel raised an eyebrow. 'No but I'll tell you what occurs to me – the fact that you immediately presume that your fancy Madame Chartreuse is telling the truth.'

'Er... she isn't my Madame Chartreuse, not by a long shot and it just seems far more probable that she is telling the truth.'

Elizabeth said, 'Now, I don't want to interfere in what seems to be the starting point of a lover's tiff, but I have to agree with Jeremy here. Your Madame Chartreuse sounds like the kind of woman who wouldn't shrink from admitting the fact, if she were having an affair with a married man. From what you've told us, her views on marriage alone seem to be quite er... how do I put it politely, well, avant-garde.'

Rachel narrowed her eyes at her mother, took a sip of her wine but said nothing.

Jeremy spoke, 'Thank you for the vote of confidence, Elizabeth. Now here's a thought for you ladies to chew on. Remember I told you that Alexandre Dubois' mistress – the one who was initially arrested for the Countess' murder, happens to have an illegitimate child. All Didier managed to wheedle out of the woman's sister was the fact that the father is Italian apparently. And now you tell me that Viola mentioned something about Pietro getting a woman into trouble...'

Rachel's eyes widened, 'No! You don't think that Pietro is the father of the child?'

'I don't think one has to be a genius to figure that out, my dear. How many Italians are involved in this case?'

'Well, it could be the Count or perhaps someone completely unrelated to the case, but somehow in this case that doesn't seem likely. And I have to admit that Pietro is quite the ladies man.'

'Yes and just the type of bloke who'd run a mile in tight shoes to avoid that kind of responsibility.'

'Jeremy!'

'My dear, where's your famous women's intuition in this case?' Jeremy chided her.

'It seems to have deserted me for now.'

Elizabeth smiled and said, 'It looks like it's been replaced by the green eyed monster instead. '

'Mums!' Rachel said in mock consternation.

'I'm your mother, dear and I can tell that there is more to your dislike of this Madame Chartreuse than you are willing to admit.'

Rachel responded, 'Well, she's the one who's been making eyes at him and as far as I know, Jeremy has been quite smug about it.'

Jeremy asked, 'What do you want me to do? Beat her off with a stick?'

'That'd be a start,' Rachel replied with a grin.

Elizabeth spoke, smiling at Rachel, 'That settles her alright. But don't you see that her interest in Jeremy is interesting by itself. Perhaps, she is telling the truth about not being romantically involved with the Count.'

'I wouldn't put it past that cat to make eyes at other men even if she were technically already in a relationship with some sorry man,' Rachel concluded in a huff, as Jeremy laughed out loud.

II

Through the night, the rain came down in sheets and covered Paris in a cold, wet blanket. Inside the room though the fire continued to burn behind the grate, lending a welcome warmth, Rachel tossed and turned in her sleep. Her body had switched off but her mind was still at work. Images and visions flooded her brain in a dream like haze. She found herself wandering through an old room full of open boxes. She walked past the boxes to an antique full length dresser mirror and saw a girl's face smiling back at her.

In the sleepy recesses of her mind she knew it was young Isabelle – the way she had looked in the black and white family picture. As she reached out with her fingertips to touch the image in the mirror, the girl magically changed into a little boy dressed in a soldier's uniform. He beckoned to her and ran towards an open door. 'Wait!' She shouted in her sleep but he was gone. There was a war going on outside. She wanted to run after him but she could hear the shells as they smashed against buildings and brought down walls. She woke up with a start.

In the light of the fire that chased the darkness away she knew without a doubt who had been telling the truth, and the knowledge brought a smile to her face. She finally knew why all the lies had been told and she knew why this person had to kill three people in order to continue fuelling a life lived on the basis of lies and deceit.

She tried to go back to sleep but it eluded her. She lay awake knowing that she would have to take the next step by herself. She still had to make sure that her assumptions were correct and there was only one way to find out. She needed some proof. She didn't want to make baseless accusations, and involve Jeremy and the police, only to find that she had made a ghastly mistake. Although she was quite sure that it was the only thing that made any sense, the only possible solution.

She got out of bed and thought of waking Jeremy up but he was in deep sleep and she placated herself that it was alright this time. All she was going to do was to see if she was right about something. She was just going to be an observer and nothing else. There was no danger in that. Not like the warehouse situation. She could take Jeremy along but something told her that it would be better and less conspicuous if she could make this journey on her own.

In the light from the fireplace she wrote Jeremy a detailed note on hotel stationary, which explained where she was going and why. It was still dark outside when she had finished writing. She sat back in the armchair and waited patiently for the morning. Then, at the first faint light of dawn, she could wait no longer and she got dressed. Jeremy's breathing was rhythmic as she took the Colt out of its box in the bureau and put it in her purse. She knew it was loaded and Jeremy had taught her how to use it a few days back. She told herself that if all went according to her plan, there would be no need for it. It was just an added precautionary measure. As she was taking out her coat, the wooden hanger fell with a thud on the floor of the wardrobe and woke Jeremy up.

'What time is it?' He asked groggily.

She switched on the bureau lamp and glanced at her watch. 'It's morning, darling. Almost 8.30 – sunrise in Paris. I'm going out for a bit. I've left a note for you.'

Jeremy groaned as he turned in his sleep, 'It's still raining and dark. Can't you go later?'

'As they say, there's no time like morning to get cracking on things, one must get done.'

He grumbled sleepily through half closed eyes, 'There's something I haven't heard from you before. A first time for everything, I suppose.' Then he yawned as he turned to his side and said, 'I'll be up in another half hour.' With that he sank deeper under the covers and went back to sleep.

Chapter Twenty Seven

A n hour and fifteen minutes later, Rachel got off at the platform of her desired destination and made her way to the tourist information desk. She waited in line behind some Americans on a day trip from Paris and when her turn came she asked the lady at the counter if she could hire a taxi preferably with a driver who could speak a smattering of English.

Twenty minutes later they had made some enquiries, which then led them towards the local forest area. The driver slowed down as he located the gates of an estate almost hidden by a grove of birch trees. She asked the driver to wait there and gave him some money. She told him that if she didn't come back in half an hour, he was to go drive back to town and call this number and tell them where she was. She handed him a paper with a name and telephone number on it. She was taking no chances this time around.

The main gate was not locked but Rachel didn't bother to open it. She noticed a small iron gate next to one of the pillars, at the entrance and she simply unlatched it and walked in. This was presumably used as a service entrance. It was wide enough to allow a bicycle in. She took the main path that led to the picturesque driveway lined with oak and birch. There were woods on either side. It was still cloudy but the rain had mercifully stopped. As the house came into view, she took the cover of the woods and skirted around it, simply walking and observing. She noticed that there were no cars or vehicles of any description on the circular gravel entrance. Then she noticed a set of outhouses and two one story buildings on her right.

The door of the first outhouse opened and she hid behind an oak tree and observed, as an old man who looked as though he was a gardener, came out of the first outhouse and walked towards the main house. He disappeared from view and she waited for five more minutes to see if anyone else was about and then she ran towards the first building. She looked through a window and saw that it was a garage. There was a car and an old van parked alongside it. She quickly made her way to the next outhouse and got the distinct smell of horse manure. She passed it and made her way to the last building.

The wooden doors were locked and as she skirted the building she realised that the windows were high up, at least ten feet above the ground. She looked about for a box to stand on but there was nothing of that description around. Then she remembered that a stable that had horses would have bales of straw. She left her handbag resting against the wall and then, as an afterthought, she removed the colt from the bag and slipped it in her coat pocket. She went back and observed that there was no one about and entered the stable. The air was warm with the smell of the animals. There were four horses in their booths. A black mare shook her head and snorted as she walked past and picked up a bale. She was surprised to find that it was quite heavy. Staggering with the weight in her arms she was glad that she had left the door open behind her. She paused for a moment at the entrance and then made her way back to the last outhouse.

She walked to the side which was facing away from the house and dumped the bale under a window. She realised that she would need another in order to reach the window but already she could hear voices in the vicinity. She stacked the bale vertically and clambered up. Although it was wobbly, from that height she could reach the window sill with her arms. She lifted herself up and to her dismay the bale of straw fell horizontally under her. In a scramble to steady herself, her foot found a foothold against the broken plaster in the wall. As she made an effort and pushing herself up, she found yet another foothold. One last heave and she was now at eye level with the window.

Despite her precarious position, Rachel's face broke into a triumphant smile. She had been right. The crates were there. Now all she had to do was drop down into the bale of straw and head back to the waiting taxi. She would drive back into town and make a telephone call. As simple as that.

Her euphoria was short lived as a familiar voice droned at her, from the rear, 'Now there's a sight one doesn't see every day!'

Despite the danger, Rachel did see the humour in that statement. She knew that to any observer she probably looked like a spider stuck on a wall.'

II

Jeremy was frantic. The car was moving too slowly for his liking. He told Didier as much. Didier spoke in French to the gendarme driving and the boy gestured back at the traffic.

Didier shook his head and said loudly, against the sounds of traffic, 'Who would have thought your wife would do it again!'

Jeremy shouted back, 'It was my bally fault that I bucked her up after what happened at the warehouse. I even gave her a gun for Dutch courage. I could kick myself.'

'Does she even know how to use it?'

'I should jolly well hope so!'

'Don't worry, my friend. Let us hope there will be no need for that.'

'What about the others?'

'Henri is making the arrests as we speak. Those officers from the Monuments Men are on their way too. But I hope this is not going to be a... how you say... chasing the wild goose.'

'I, on the other hand, pray that it she is on a wild goose chase and that she's safe. As far as I'm concerned, I no longer care about the murders. I'm putting her on the next train to England with her mother for company.'

III

Rachel was facing her adversary who was holding a hunting rifle pointed at her. After she had fallen from the window to the bale of straw, the rifle had been a compelling argument to do as she was told. She was made to walk towards the main house with her hands up. Five minutes later, they stood facing each other in the main sitting room where all the furniture was covered in dust sheets.

'When did you know?'

Rachel answered, 'Early this morning. I realised that one of you was lying and then it came to me that it had to be you.'

'Go on.'

'Well. You made the mistake of telling me one extra needless lie,' Rachel said.

'What was that?'

'You led me to believe that Pietro had fathered Suzette's boy. He couldn't have, you see because the boy is five and Pietro only came to Paris four years ago. He was in Italy before that and there is no indication that Suzette ever left France during the war. It was your lover, the Count who had fathered the child when he was allegedly working for the Resistance. Oh, yes. I am sure it won't take us long to find out that he has fascist alliances. You and your friend von Schmidt for instance.'

'Ah! I see. And you think he killed his wife as well?'

'No, Madame Chartreuse. You killed her because she stumbled upon your profession quite by chance and would not have hesitated to throw you to the wolves; the woman who had destroyed her marriage.'

'It was her fault, she couldn't hold on to her husband, or mind her own business and Aaron's stupidity in offering her the Vermeer. But he wasn't to know that she would get a second opinion from that ninny, Isabelle.

'Yes, interestingly enough, the Count tried to throw us off the scent. He gave us a cooked up a story about a Rembrandt when it had been the Vermeer all along. Isabelle instantly recognised the painting and told Sarah. Though, I still don't know how Sarah or Isabelle learnt that you were the supplier. You kept your profession so well hidden for the past few years.'

'That was Aaron's second mistake. He insisted that it could not have been a stolen painting because it had come from my estate and he trusted me. Once I killed Sarah, Isabelle started digging to find out where Aaron had got that painting from, and he told her as well.'

'Are you telling me that for all his worldliness Aaron did not have a clue that you were involved with this group of Nazis? Even after the two women who knew the truth were found murdered?'

'No, he really did believe that I was selling paintings from my own estates to help make up for the crippling death duties. Perhaps he wanted them so badly that he forced himself to believe it. And he took it upon himself that he would not reveal the fact to society that I was in a terrible financial situation. He was kindness itself.'

'A shrewd sort of kindness that benefitted enormously from all the masters he sold from "your collection". But he had no choice but to give away your game, when the Countess approached him all guns blazing. Yes, you like to let it be known that your wealth came from your late husband but the reality is that there wasn't much left when he died, was there? Just a lot of estates and no money to run them. And yet appearances had to be maintained.'

'You are sharp, I must admit. Yes, my fool of a husband speculated in war bonds and left me with nothing. It is through my own industry that I am a wealthy woman today.'

'Wealth without work, I'm afraid, never gets you very far.'

'Save your sermons for your next life, my dear. You have so little time left in this one.'

'We shall see. You can kill me but this time you won't get away with it.'

'My dear, I have gotten away with two. The third will be a charm.'

'Wait a minute. Just two? Who killed Pierre then?'

'Oh! I'm surprised that the great English detective hasn't figured that out.'

Rachel rolled her eyes, 'But of course, it was the Count. Who else would've known, apart from Aaron himself that the sword was real! Aaron would have informed him when he bought that warrior. But why? Why would he kill Pierre?'

'Because the fool stumbled upon the truth after I killed Isabelle. He was blackmailing me. Tristan only did it to protect me.'

'Pietro was right on all counts – he told me that you both were made for each other and as cold hearted as snakes.'

'That is enough.'

'Do you know you are in love with a man who is willing to frame his own brother for murder?'

'That was my idea. Why do you think I slit their throats when I could have just as easily stabbed them?'

Rachel answered slowly, 'To make it look as though a man had committed the murders. That explains the veronal.'

'And why do you think that Tristan hired you?'

'Quite obviously to frame Pietro but he underestimated us. That was his mistake.'

'A mistake he will correct shortly. Now, move. I have telephoned Tristan and he is on his way here. We will decide what to do with you, once he gets here.'

'You mean how to kill me. Must plan it well. Perhaps slit my throat and put my body in Pietro's lodging.'

'That is a fine idea. Ah, that must be him,' she said, as they heard a car drive up.

As Madame Chartreuse momentarily took her eyes off her victim, to look out of the window, Rachel slipped her hand into her coat pocket brought out the colt, released the safety, aimed and fired. It all happened within seconds.

Madame Chartreuse was on the ground screaming with pain. The bullet had smashed her right elbow and flung the rifle she was holding out of her hand.

Rachel moved quickly and kicked it further out of her reach and told her, 'Damn and blast! I was aiming for your hand. I won't hesitate to use it again and as you can see, I'm not a very good shot. If you wriggle too much, I may just end up shooting you in the head if I aim for your feet. So be still.'

She craned her neck and saw Jeremy and Didier step out of the car on the driveway. Waves of relief flooded over her. She had always liked the sight of Jeremy but she never realised that she would be just as pleased to see the little Napoleon as well.

Epilogue

The double arrest made waves in Paris. Henri Beauchamp had arrested Count Santinelli in Paris just as he was about to leave for Compiègne, while Didier had made the second and more notorious arrest of Madame Chartreuse, now nicknamed the "black widow" by the French newspapers.

Rachel and Jeremy got flattering mentions in most of the newspaper articles and Rachel especially was made out to be quite the heroine. Amidst all the applause, she made a silent promise to herself that she had to seriously work on her target practice for future cases.

When faced with murder charges both the Count and Madame Chartreuse began to sing like canaries in a coal mine and gave full confessions to the police, each trying to pin the idea behind the crimes on the other.

Aaron Berger was released from the murder charge but now faced fresh charges of aiding and abetting war criminals by dealing in stolen paintings. The Rosenheims appointed a top notch lawyer for him, who had appealed that bail be granted for the lesser charges. It was approved and Aaron was reinstated in the comfort of his home once more. Rachel and Jeremy attended a small soiree at his house along with Elizabeth Markham and the Rosenheims on the evening of his release. Pietro was there too and Rachel was happy to note that despite his brother's terrible betrayal, his signature charm was still intact.

The Monuments Men revealed that they had recovered hundreds of stolen paintings, sculptures and antiques from the crates that were moved from the warehouse at Montmartre and hidden in Madame Chartreuse's estate in Compiègne. Madame Chartreuse had also given a statement that she was only the go-between and that she was the recipient of only twenty percent of the total sale value of the artwork and that the remaining eighty percent was handed over to the Northern Cargo Company. Based on this revelation, an official investigation was launched into Freidrich von Schmidt's art collection and his links to Nazi war criminals – an investigation that would eventually lead to finding some of the most wanted Nazi criminals who had gone into hiding in Argentina.

Out of the two hundred and sixty crates, fifteen crates containing treasures robbed from the Rosenheims during the war, were returned to Prudence and Jonathan Rosenheim. The Vermeer was also handed back to them in a special ceremony at Jeu de Paume. With what they had recovered, the Rosenheims could finally invest in an apartment of their own in Paris.

Suzette Bouvier was brought back to Paris and revealed that she had received the payout from Countess Santinelli just before she was murdered in exchange for the testimony she had agreed to give in the forth coming divorce proceedings against Count Santinelli. Suzette told Didier that the Countess had approached her and beseeched her to reveal the truth of Etienne's paternity so that she would have a solid ground for divorce from the Count.

When asked why she had fled to Dordogne, she revealed that when Pierre Lambert had approached her with his knowledge about the murders and asked her if she knew anything about the Count's involvement in them, she had panicked and assumed that the Count had murdered the Countess and would come after her too, if he knew that she had been ready to testify on the Countess' behalf. And that had been the reason that she had feared for her and her son's safety and had gone into hiding at Dordogne.

Anna Marie and Didier started seeing each other seriously and the standing joke at the Sûreté was that the little Napoleon had finally found his Joséphine. The aroma of delicious baked goods that found their way into La Crim at regular intervals soon quelled the dissenters and the jokes shifted to Didier's expanding waistline instead.

Elizabeth, Rachel and Jeremy were back at Rutherford Hall just in time for Christmas with a genuine Vermeer that Elizabeth had purchased from her friends – the Rosenheims. The Masterpiece was given pride of place in the main gallery where family and friends could view it and recount the momentous events in Paris that preceded its arrival at Rutherford Hall. It was after all a very well traveled painting that not only helped in solving three murders but it had also travelled half way across the world, survived two World Wars and the Nazis, to boot!

15774999R00133

Made in the USA
Middletown, DE
20 November 2014